THE LAST CHANGELING

Books by
JANE YOLEN

Young Merlin Trilogy
Passager
Hobby
Merlin

The Pit Dragon Chronicles
Dragon's Blood
Heart's Blood
A Sending of Dragons
Dragon's Heart

Sword of the Rightful King
The Last Dragon
Curse of the Thirteenth Fey
Snow in Summer
Dragon's Boy
Sister Light, Sister Dark
White Jenna
The One-Armed Queen
Wild Hunt
Wizard's Hall
Boots and the Seven Leaguers

THE LAST CHANGELING

THE SEELIE WARS: BOOK II

Jane Yolen & Adam Stemple

VIKING

An imprint of Penguin Group (USA)

VIKING
Published by the Penguin Group
Penguin Group (USA) LLC
375 Hudson Street
New York, New York 10014

USA / Canada / UK / Ireland / Australia
New Zealand / India / South Africa / China

penguin.com
A Penguin Random House Company

First published in the United States of America by Viking,
an imprint of Penguin Group (USA) LLC, 2015

LIBRARY OF CONGRESS CATALOGING-IN-PUBLICATION DATA IS AVAILABLE
ISBN 978-0-670-01435-4

Printed in USA

1   3   5   7   9   10   8   6   4   2

Designed by Eileen Y. Savage
Set in Galliard

Penguin
Random
House

For Alison, David, and Betsy because they couldn't wait for the second book—J.Y.

For Alex, who lives on, forever young—A.S.

CONTENTS

THE LAST
CHANGELING

SNAIL ON THE ROAD

*S*nail's new clothes itched. The soft wool of the mauve gown seemed to set her skin on fire. Running a finger under the top of the bodice, she thought about how she must look. The neckline was too low, the hemline too high, the lace collar too starched. There was no apprentice over-apron with deep pockets like the one she'd worn all her working life. She missed those pockets. *You could keep a sticky bun or a knife or an apple or a hair ribbon or a comb there. Or, if you had a coin . . .*

And then she thought angrily, *Toffs probably have no need of pockets. If you're rich enough, someone carries all your stuff for you.* Well, she wasn't a toff, just a midwife's apprentice. *A midwife's apprentice,* she reminded herself, *on the run with a hostage prince. And both of us being sought by not one but two armies. TWO!*

She said "TWO!" out loud, and it sounded like an explosion, the kind wizards make with smoke and fire and a horrible stench.

And how can I possibly run from any armies in these shoes? She glared at her feet. An hour earlier, her midwife sandals, well broken in and comfortable, had entered into an unfortunate battle with a peat bog. They'd lost. *Or rather*, she thought, *they'd* been *lost*.

She'd had to put on the shoes the queen had given her, the ones that she'd been carrying for miles slung around her neck by their laces. With their narrow toes and small heels, they pinched her feet. She'd known at once that they weren't the kind of shoes made for long walks across treacherous terrain. They were dancing shoes made for a grand ball. And *that* was a terrain she'd never crossed in her life, nor did she ever want to.

The fancy dress made her feel . . . *exposed* was the word that leapt to mind. *Vulnerable. Visible.*

As a midwife's apprentice she'd worn a uniform that both identified her and made her part of a team. She was a pair of hands, a ready heart, an agile mind, but otherwise invisible. At least that's what Mistress Softhands—who's apprentice she'd been—had always said.

But poor Mistress Softhands was in the dungeon of the Unseelie castle now, completely invisible to everyone except the guards. Her partners—Mistress Treetop and Mistress Yoke—were there as well. And the other midwife's apprentice, Yarrow.

Actually, Snail didn't care a fyge about Yarrow. *Let her scream her lungs out in that place!* she thought with a bitterness that surprised her. But Mistress Softhands had been a good teacher, if strict. Her only mother, indeed her only trustworthy friend in the beastly Unseelie Court, as she understood now. Even though she'd learned from the other midwives as well, they'd never been a particularly comforting lot. Yes, they'd imparted knowledge with their every breath, but they imparted as well a certain heartlessness, a nasty preference for their own apprentices whether the girls had been worthy or not. She shuddered, remembering. Still, the knowledge of midwifery had helped in her endless escape from the Unseelie lands.

Well, not endless, she quickly amended to herself. *It's only been a couple of days.*

"But they were awful days. . . ." she mumbled. "Beatings and a death and a stay in the Unseelie dungeon and . . ."

"Really," Aspen said beside her, "can you not . . . er . . . *can't* you say something pleasant?"

She glared at him and then thought, *Well, there weren't any actual beatings, only a bit of manhandling—but I probably have bruises. He wouldn't want me to mention those. And there was a dungeon. And two, no three . . . no five or six deaths, if you count the ogre who was questioning me and the two assassins, and Philomel, the apprentice midwife. Oh, and three or four Border Lords eaten by carnivorous mermen. And the merman I stabbed with a poisoned blade. Maybe that was eight or nine deaths. Or ten. Nothing pleasant there!*

The merman had been the only one she herself had killed.

Snail could almost feel his cold, wet fingers around her body as he tried to drag her from the boat. She shuddered again.

Still, she'd delivered a baby along the way. A troll's baby. The first she'd ever done unsupervised and all by herself. And she hadn't dropped it or been eaten in the process. Maybe that balanced everything out. Maybe she could remind Prince High-and-Holy Aspen—Karl!—of that. After all, it was a very *big* baby. Once again, she blessed whoever had made the law that forbade trolls to eat midwives.

But the other midwives had been left behind in the dungeon, and Snail was now running for her life across Seelie lands, the Hostage Prince by her side.

They'd already crossed fields and those soft, peaty bogs that threatened to grab them and pull them under. The Peat Hags—so Mistress Softhands had once warned—were merciless and cunning old things, notorious for their greed. She said their teeth were enormous and sharp as a chef's knife. Snail was glad she'd only lost the shoes in the bog and not her feet as well.

But to be honest, Snail thought, *we only encountered mud, not hags. And beyond the bogs were well-tended farms with the barley halfway up to our thighs, and corn, too. Some grouse leapt up when we passed, which was scary—all that loud wing-fluttering—but no one seemed to notice us.*

And here we are, wherever here *is!* She hoped Prince Aspen—who was Seelie and had lived his first seven years in the Seelie kingdom they were now traveling in before he'd been sent off as the Hostage Prince—still remembered his way around. She'd never been anywhere outside the Unseelie castle till their escape. Wasn't sure yet that travel was a good thing, under the circumstances.

They'd already crossed two streams, leaping from rock to rock, not daring to wade in the water. *Thank Mab the rivers had been too shallow for merfolk.* Her stomach had remarked about trout, but she doubted the prince knew how to fish. *And I'm no cook. Though at least with his fire magic we could have tried.*

Aspen had claimed—with more authority than knowledge—that the mer lived only in salt water. Snail hadn't felt it necessary to remind him that the great river they'd so recently crossed by boat into the Seelie lands had been fresh water and not salt. *And full of carnivorous mer.*

Still, the two of them were free.

Free!

Or as free as they could be with two armies chasing them—Seelie and Unseelie.

Snail made a face and pulled on a strand of her red-orange hair.

Free maybe, but far too identifiable when they should be trying to remain invisible.

No one, she thought miserably, *can be invisible in these clothes.* She pulled up on the bodice again. Ran her finger around the starched collar again. Bit her lower lip in frustration.

The prince—she had to remember to call him Karl, his minstrel name—*looks even stranger than me in his multi-colored rags and silly red hat.* She feared the two of them stuck out like apples on a winter tree, like dog meat at the king's high table . . . like . . .

She must have said that last aloud because the prince—Karl—asked, "Why dog meat? Cannot . . . er . . . *can't* you think of . . ."

"Something more pleasing?"

"Exactly."

Snail shrugged but didn't otherwise answer him. Right now, they needed what breath they had for running, hiding, being invisible, not wasting it with talking. They needed minds that were devious and serious and alert and questioning. Not minds that were worried about pleasing things. Or pleasing people.

Besides, even while trying so hard to be an ordinary person—his golden hair hidden under a scruffy hat, his voice harsh from his ordeal, carefully saying "can't" instead of "cannot" and "I'm" instead of "I am"—Prince Aspen still looked and sounded like a toff.

It's all hopeless, really. And by Mab's little toe, this bodice itches! Snail was miserable. She expected soon to be covered in a roseate rash, as raw as a baby's bottom, probably by nightfall. And probably locked up in another dungeon as well.

The problem was that in these clothes they weren't disguised at all. In fact, they were *highly* visible. And not only were they visible, now they were on a main road.

A main road with very few people so far—only a couple of rough peasants had passed them by, and never gave them a second glance. The lack of people who might be curious or able to identify them had only been by luck. After all, it was early morning, the light was a dull grey, like pewter, rain threatened, and until now they'd been walking in fields and bogs and wasteland, so it wasn't a surprise that they hadn't yet been noticed.

"Pleasing?" she said again, or rather whispered it, though the whisper was almost as loud as a shout. "You want me to think of something *pleasing*? When every step along a road like this brings us danger and possible imprisonment, probably death? How about my being back in the Unseelie Court working side by side with the other midwives, hands bloody from bringing a child into the world. It would be a sight more *pleasing* than this." She gestured toward the bodice, the skirt, the shoes.

"I think you look . . ." Aspen hesitated.

"Yes?" Now she stood, hands on hips, as if daring him to figure his way out of this small predicament in the middle of their much greater one.

All the while she wondered if he was going to say she looked like a sow in a princess's castoff, which in a way she was. Or a toad before it was kissed by the prince, as the old story went. Or . . . she shuddered at the idea of kissing a prince. It could be a hanging offense.

"Um . . . pleasing." He shrugged, tried to grin, failing that, looked faintly embarrassed, before getting angry, shifting the lute—with its battered carving of a cross-eyed cherub—behind him and folding his arms. He all but growled at her. "Girls!"

She liked him angry. It would make him more careful the next time. It would make him . . .

He looked past her, down the road, then suddenly flung himself prone onto the ground, right ear dramatically against the road. Then just as dramatically, he sat up and pointed.

"Horses!" he said. "Probably soldiers. Quick—the trees."

But she was already running. She hadn't needed to put *her* ear to the ground to hear the horses. That many horses make a lot of noise. And that many horses meant soldiers. It mattered little to Snail if the soldiers were Seelie or Unseelie because it meant death to the two of them either way.

Aspen was right behind her, and at the last, when they were in a rough patch of grass about ten steps from the trees, he tackled her and they both went down in a flurry of her skirts, and his silly red hat flew into the air.

"What did you do that for?" she said, glaring at him.

"Stay down," he said. "The grass will hide us. It is our only chance. We were never going to make it to the trees."

She looked about carefully and could see he was right.

They lay there for a very long time, hardly moving, till the sound of the horses was entirely gone. In fact they both fell asleep for a while, fear and exhaustion combining with the constant birdsong—wrens and cuckoos calling above them working as well as any sleep potion.

❖ ❖ ❖

WAKING LATER WITH a start, Snail realized her dress was now itchier than before because the grass had gotten down the front of the bodice and she had had to pinch her nose with her right hand to keep from sneezing, in case anyone was about.

The sun had begun its descent when they sat up, both at the same time. Carefully, looking around and seeing the road once again deserted, they stood and straightened themselves out, brushing bits of grass and seeds and brambles from their clothes—*to look half-decent*, Mistress Softhands would have said.

Then they argued a bit, looking for the red hat, but never finding it, which was strange.

"Maybe a bogle took it," the prince said. "Or a brownie."

"This far from a house?" All she knew about brownies was what she'd heard in travelers' tales. Brownies were Seelie folk, small servants who kept the home, hard workers, though not thought to be terribly smart.

His face looked as if an argument was about to start, but before he could correct her, he breathed out a single word.

"Bother!"

They turned at the same time.

Snail thought, *Entirely visible.* Meaning herself. Meaning the prince.

But not, perhaps, as visible as the cart.

She knew it was too late to run from it, but that didn't stop her from trying. What really stopped her, though, was Prince Aspen's hand. He caught her upper arm roughly and held on.

I've been princed! she thought, which was something everyone said when a toff decided to lay a hand on an underling. There was something, especially in a mature prince's hand, that could burn at a touch. Though she did wonder if Prince Aspen was mature enough for that. *Either way, I'll wear bruises the size and shape of his fingers tomorrow.*

The cart was the oddest contraption Snail had ever seen and was as long as five or six regular market carts. The sides had brass latches so they could fold down, though for what reason Snail couldn't guess. A solid roof arched over the wagon—or rather four arched roofs about eight feet high—and there were twelve large wooden wheels, six on each side. It made the cart look top-heavy, like a moving mill, and yet somehow it all worked.

The cart was pulled by four huge, gleaming white war horses, their feet feathered with thick hair.

Snail quickly corrected herself when she saw that each horse had a stiff, whorled horn in the center of its forehead.

"War unicorns?" she whispered to the prince.

He shrugged. Shook his head. Either he meant he'd never seen any such either, or else they were a specialty of the Seelie kingdom. Either way, they were amazing.

As the cart came closer, she could make out three dwarfs—siblings by the look of them—sitting on a raised platform at the front, reins in their hands. *Two males and a female*, she thought, though of course they all had beards, so she could have been wrong.

"Players," the prince said. *Karl*, she reminded herself. "Just ordinary players."

The only players she'd ever seen at the Unseelie Court had been a motley crew of five who'd arrived at the castle in a small green wagon and done a sloppy performance of "Dread Ned the Pirate King" for the apprentices with a lot of whoops and dancing to cover the forgotten or misspoken lines. Their horrendous attempt at performing "The Fairy Revels" for the court had almost gotten them eaten by the drows.

"Here's our chance," Karl said, letting go of her arm.

"Chance?" She wondered if she was being thick.

A moment later, the wagon went by them, its side covered with posters about the troupe written in garish colors proclaiming that Professor Odds and His Magnificent Players had performed before kings and commoners alike.

That's when Snail understood Aspen's meaning.

He held out his hand. "Come on!"

"No!" Snail said. "No, no, no!" Players were meant to be seen. The only way she and the prince were going to escape capture was to remain invisible. "No! No! No!"

"*That* is the perfect hiding place for us," he said.

She put her hand in his. For the life of her—*and probably the death of me, too*, she thought—she didn't know why.

2

ASPEN HAILS THE WAGON

*A*s they scampered to catch up with the rumbling cart, Aspen tried to explain his half-formed idea to Snail.

"The armies will be looking for hiders," he said, "so we should not . . . er . . . shouldn't hide!"

Snail gave him a look usually reserved for feast hounds that threw up on the banquet table. Or an apprentice midwife who dropped a blanket or a baby.

He tried again. "The hooded face, the concealing cloak, the furtive movement, the swift turning away—these are what will attract the soldiers' eyes." He pointed at the gaudy cart. "But what fugitives in their right minds would stand on a stage and perform for all to see?"

"I doubt anyone ever accused you of being in your right mind," Snail said. But she showed him a brief smile, and he thought that perhaps she understood his point.

"Good, we are—we're—in agreement then."

"Oh, I wouldn't say that," Snail said. "But I agree that your idea makes a certain amount of crazy sense." She glanced ahead at the cart, which had slowed to a bare walking pace to deal with deep ruts in the road. "But why would they take us on?"

Aspen grinned and said nothing until they were just a few feet behind the cart. "Listen."

Snail wrinkled her nose as she concentrated on her hearing. "I don't hear anything."

"Exactly," Aspen said mysteriously. Then, "Ow!" as Snail squeezed his hand hard.

"What am I supposed to hear?" she hissed.

Aspen wrenched his hand free and peevishly answered with another question. "What always accompanies a player's performance?"

He watched her contemplate that for a few moments—or more likely contemplate which of his limbs she could reach with a kick—before realizing that Snail had probably never seen a *decent* performance by a group of players. Troupes of fine actors and acrobats and artisans and performers of all kinds were constantly seeking audience at court, leaving their apprentices to perform for the underlings. He suddenly felt sorrow for Snail, but then she *was* of a different station in life than he, and nothing was ever going to be able to bring her closer.

A different everything! he thought. But it didn't seem to matter as much as it had when they first met. When his life had made sense. *Actually,* he reminded himself, *it had been a horrible life. Being a hostage prince was full of dangerous pitfalls and enemies at every turn. But it* had *made sense.*

Now nothing made sense. Not only had he been tricked into starting a war, but his father—his real father—wanted him executed for treason, his mother wanted him dressed as a minstrel, and there were two armies actively looking for him. And, to make matters worse, he had just insulted his only friend (who was a servant, of all things), and he did not know how to apologize, because he should not *have* to apologize. He was a prince and she was a midwife, and he could insult her all he wanted without fear of anyone thinking he had done wrong.

Only now I am no longer a prince—I'm Karl the minstrel and she has saved my life as I have saved hers, and . . .

Aspen tried desperately to think of a way to take back the insult—such as it was—to roll back the clock two minutes and close his fool mouth before speaking again.

"Music," Snail said, snapping the fingers of her free hand.

"Exactly!" Aspen gushed with relief. "And we know they have none because their only practice time is while they travel. We would hear them playing." As a child, having escaped from the nursemaid, he would climb the walls of the palace to watch the players approach because he so loved hearing music skirling from the wagons as the musicians put the finishing touches on the evening's performances.

This wagon was deathly silent.

"Halloo the players!" Aspen called as they drew even with the dwarfs on the front seat.

"Asp—Karl, no!" Snail cried in a desperate whisper, but she was too late.

The lead unicorn on the right turned its head slightly, though it kept on walking, but the others plodded on as if Aspen had not spoken at all.

The middle dwarf, slightly taller than the other two and possibly female, smiled and called back, "Halloo the ground!"

Aspen chuckled politely. "I . . . can't . . . help but notice you're without musical accompaniment." He was proud of not sounding like a toff for an entire sentence. Dropping Snail's hand, he swung his lute off his back with a theatrical flourish, saying, "I, Karl the minstrel, wish to offer my . . ." His words petered out as he realized the dwarfs were no longer listening to him. They were staring past him at Snail.

When she realized they were staring, she, of course, took up a belligerent stance, hands on hips, chin jutted out. "What are *you* looking at?"

Oh no, Aspen thought, *they have recognized us.*

The dwarfs exchanged a few brief words in their native tongue.

Aspen's knowledge of Dwarfish was limited and rusty, for he had had little chance to practice it in the Unseelie Court. Dwarfs were not common there. They were Seelie folk, and what he knew of their language came from the first few years of his childhood when one of his father's jesters had been a dwarf. Even so, he caught two words: skarm drema. He was fairly certain that meant "free one."

Or maybe what they said was "liberated body." Dwarfish had very few words and so each word had at least three close but not equal meanings. And sometimes one or more oppositional meanings as well. They might have also meant "tied woman," or "newlywed." His nurse, when he had been a prince of the Seelie, had been quite specific. "It's tone that counts," she had said often enough. However, these dwarfs had been speaking too quickly and quietly for Aspen to get their meaning.

But whatever they had meant, all three of them pulled on the reins at the same time, and the giant unicorns came to a quick halt, the lead one stomping impatiently in its traces, giant hooves making dust winds swirl around the front wagon wheels.

None of the dwarfs were smiling anymore.

"Girl," the middle dwarf said to Snail, "Professor Odds will want to see you. Hop to, before the soldiers return."

Aspen moved quickly to put himself between Snail and the dwarfs, his hand moving to his hip for a sword that no longer hung there. He tried to remember where he'd hidden his dagger in his ridiculous minstrel costume but stopped when he realized he was patting himself randomly and probably looking like a buffoon. So he puffed his chest and tried to regain his dignity with a brave speech.

"Who is this Professor Odds and why should I allow him to see her? Perhaps we should be wary of him and not some paltry soldiery." He was feeling fairly proud of his performance until Snail pushed past him and tapped the side of the cart.

"He's the leader of the company, genius," she said. "It says so right there."

The script on the cart's side was quite flowery. It wrapped around a painting of an oddly jointed silver spider who seemed to be proclaiming that the cart contained "Professor Odds's Traveling Circus of Works & Wonders, Performance & Prestidigitation, with Occasional Flights of Fancy & Fantasy, Not to Mention a Marvel of Mimicry and Action." The last was in smaller letters, but still readable.

Aspen muttered, "So it does," and feeling the fool, followed meekly behind Snail as the three dwarfs hopped nimbly from their perch and led her to the back of the wagon.

SNAIL ENTERS THE WAGON

$\mathscr{F}$rom behind it was even harder to tell the dwarfs apart, as they dressed alike in rust-red thigh-length tunics and brown hose. They were shoeless and their feet looked hard as shod hoofs.

In the back of the wagon was a round door—rather like the entrance to a cave. It yawned open.

"You are expected," said the tallest of the dwarfs, turning to Snail and grinning. There seemed to be genuine delight in the smile, as well as too few teeth. No doubt knocked out in a pub fight. That marked this dwarf as the female. The males rarely fought except in times of war.

"How could I be expected?" Snail asked. "If I didn't know I was coming upon you, how could anyone else?"

The dwarf woman giggled, which made her beard move back and forth. "Magic!" she said, waggling her fingers, and pushing Snail up the two steps.

The door snicked shut behind her, and Snail was instantly

worried. She was now inside the mysterious cart. Aspen and the three dwarfs were on the outside. It could be a trap. The only other time she and the prince had been separated on their escape journey had been when he'd been led off to his execution.

Well, she thought, *that didn't work then. Maybe this won't work now.*

Whatever this *is.*

That thought didn't make her any less afraid.

Slowly her eyes adjusted to the gloom of the room. There were two lanterns, one on either wall, but they were too feeble to be doing much of a job. She could only barely make out two long beds, one on either side of the room and a single tall table in the middle. Stepping forward carefully to avoid the table, she tripped over something large and furry on the floor, only just managing to right herself by grabbing the nearby bedstead.

The furry thing yelped, sat up, and showed about a hundred white teeth. Before Snail could scream, the mouth shut, the teeth were hidden, and presumably the creature—whatever its pedigree—lay back down again.

"Not much of a watch hound," she whispered to give herself courage.

"Why would we need a watch hound?" came a voice at her ear.

She whipped around and stared into the gloom but could see nothing. She was preparing to shout for help when a being in a long black cape materialized out of the gloaming, its two pupil-less eyes staring at her. "We have nothing worth stealing here."

"I . . . I . . ." Snail stuttered. "I was sent in by the dwarfs."

"They prefer we call them Little Folk." The voice came from an unseen mouth, located, Snail presumed, somewhere below the two staring eyes, though the cape and the lack of light—and perhaps, she thought hopefully, the lack of teeth—hid the mouth from her.

"All right," Snail said. "Little Folk. I'll remember that." She looked behind her, trying to locate the door. It, too, was lost in the darkness.

"Skarm drema?" the creature asked.

They were the same words the dwarfs had used before. But as Snail only knew *skrek!*, which was what dwarfs— Little Folk—said to get your attention or to ask for berry beer or for pain relief in the midst of giving birth, she'd no idea what the creature meant.

She'd had very little to do with dwarfs actually—just helped out at one dwarf woman's labor, which had been the very first time she'd been allowed in a birthing room. It was the one babe she'd ever dropped. Luckily onto the bed. But none of the midwives had ever let her forget it. Since there were very few dwarfs in the Unseelie Court—and those few brought back by the Border Lords after raids in the Seelie kingdom and made to serve as jesters and fools—it wasn't a language she'd ever had much need to learn.

"Maybe I am *skarm drema*," she said, hoping it was the right answer and not a swear.

"The professor will know," said the cloaked creature, and pointed to the next room.

Snail squinted in that direction, noticing at the same time that the creature's hand was thin and pale, as if it were something that had been long under a rock that had only just now been turned over. The fingers were much like knobbed sticks, the nails either naturally white or painted.

"That way," the voice said, a bit ghostly, a lot scary.

Snail understood. She was to go through to the next room. There would be no turning back to find the door to outside.

Just pretend, she told herself, *that you are a babe in the womb hurtling down the birth canal and heading for the light.* Unfortunately, it wasn't a particularly comforting thought as she moved toward the door.

❖ ❖ ❖

MAKING HER WAY forward with a bit more care, wondering all the while if she was a prisoner—or a guest—Snail was pleased that at least she fell over no other furry creature on the way.

At last she reached the door, pushed it open, stepped over the small lintel, and found herself in a brighter room. Here three lanterns glowed merrily. There were three beds as well, all set against the wall on the right, each one small enough for a child.

Or a dwarf, she thought. *Little Folk.*

The room was a tumble of mismatched chairs and small tables, large pillows on the floor, and an assortment of toys that looked rather worn as if something with teeth had played with them. She picked her way slowly through the toys.

A sudden squawk from her left made her turn. In a cage, swinging on a perch, was some sort of bird, with a long tail and a curved beak like a sword. The color of the tail seemed to be a cross between pink and blood red.

"Feed the troll," said the bird in a sharp, high voice.

"You're not a troll," Snail snapped.

"Pay the toll," the bird said.

"This is not a road," Snail answered. Then, not wanting to be bested by a bird, she spit out the dwarf's words, "Skarm drema!" She probably mangled it. But maybe not.

The bird responded at once, squawking out, "Skarm drema!" three times, and the door at the far end of the room opened.

When Snail hesitated, the bird said, as if continuing their previous conversation, "If it winds, it's a road." It cawed, then said again, this time in a failing voice, "Skarm drema— if it winds, it's a road." It repeated the same sentence a third time as if running out of ideas, then ended with a pitiful moan.

"If it whines, it's a bird," Snail said, squaring her shoulders before going through the door. She would have preferred talking to the dwarfs, strange as they were. Or the cloaked creature. Or even the thing with teeth on the floor. She certainly didn't want to wait around to hear any next line from the bird.

ASPEN AND THE DWARFS

*A*spen stared at the closed door and then at the three dwarfs, wondering if he should go in after Snail. Separation was not a good idea. The last time they had been separated . . .

The dwarfs stared back.

Rather rudely, he thought. But then he reminded himself that he wasn't a prince anymore, and anyone could stare at a minstrel as rudely as they wanted and expect no punishment for it. In fact, he supposed, getting stared at was an essential part of a minstrel's job. Stared at and listened to. Two things he was definitely not accustomed to after his years as a hostage in the Unseelie Court. There, if anyone responded to him at all, it had usually been with derision, mockery, or laughter.

Of course, he thought, *maybe that was what was going on here as well.*

"Ummm." He inclined his head toward the closed door.

The taller dwarf spit through its teeth—or the place where some teeth would have been—and said nothing. The sputum was green, the color of those little worms that turned into flutterbys with their sharp teeth and barbed wings.

Grimacing, Aspen wondered what possible foodstuff could turn saliva that particular shade of green. He decided not to ask that but rather to answer rudeness with courtesy.

"My dear lady," he said while giving a small bow. Up close he was now certain the taller dwarf was female. There was a fineness to her cheekbones—well, the parts of her cheekbones that weren't covered by her beard—and a thinness to her nose. There were also the missing teeth. Female dwarfs were incorrigible brawlers.

"My dear lady, I wish to enter your . . . um . . . noble . . . carriage and join my traveling companion. If you and your brethren could please step aside."

Her eyebrow rose at "My dear lady," but the frown never left her face. She drew in a breath through her nose and Aspen took an involuntary step back, fearful she was going to spit again. Or worse.

"No," she said.

"I must insist you step aside!" Aspen said, bristling. *Really, how much insolence must I take from these . . .*

His thoughts ran down as he realized once again that he was no longer a prince and he no longer carried a sword.

The female dwarf, far from looking intimidated, was finally smiling once more. She cracked her knuckles while the two males, still looking grim, let their hands drift toward their belts and the well-worn hand axes that hung from them.

"Insist away, popinjay," she said. Aspen towered over her, but he couldn't help noticing how broad her shoulders were and how thick her fists. Her ears, too, were swollen and misshapen, as if she'd spent a lifetime in and out of wrestling holds.

Lovely, Aspen thought. *I am about to be beaten bloody by a creature I could step over.*

"Now, let us reconsider," he said quickly, then remembering a minstrel shouldn't sound like a prince, changed it to "I mean, let's hold on a moment."

If anything, the female's grin grew wider and she took a step toward him. "Why?"

"Because . . ." Aspen began, but stopped and thought, *Yes, because why? They owe you no allegiance. No one does. Because of you, thousands of innocent Seelie folk will probably be slaughtered. And thousands of Unseelie, too. Though that wouldn't be such a disaster. Except for the innocents, like the midwives. And the potboys. And my tutor, Jaunty. And . . .* He bit his lower lip, thinking, *You are reviled in both lands, and rightfully so. The only person in all the realms who likes you even a little is . . .*

"Snail," he said.

"Because . . . Snail?" the female mocked him, then guffawed heartily. "The air thin up there, elfling?"

Aspen shook his head, half in answer and half to clear it. "No, I . . . it's just . . ."

"Yes?"

He took a deep breath and gathered himself. *Obviously no manners or courtesy will work here.* He took another peek at the female dwarf's cabbage ears. His right hand pawed reflexively at the spot on his belt where his sword would normally hang. *And violence is right out, too.* Sighing, he straightened his back and tugged the hem of his jacket straight. *If I am to be bludgeoned to death, I will carry it off as nobly as possible.* "It is just that the only friend left to me in all the world is now inside that wagon."

The female's grin waned as he continued.

"And you can mock me, or beat me, or even kill me." He put a brave foot forward. *Well, not an actual foot, more like a toe.* "But you cannot keep me from her."

The dwarf's grin left her face entirely, but she didn't move out of the way. Aspen took a full step forward and steeled himself to walk over or through or around her.

Brave words, he thought, *but putting them to action is going to be another thing altogether.*

He gulped and had just lifted the toes of his right foot off the ground when one of the male dwarfs spoke.

"Skrek!"

Aspen thought that meant "Listen up!" Or "Halt!"

"Brave words," the dwarf said, as if reading Aspen's mind, "and bravely spoken." He turned to the female. "The professor would like those words."

The other male chimed in. "Put them in one of his plays, he would."

"He's a fine one with the words is the professor," said the first.

"Not like our sister, Dagmarra," said the second.

"She's a fine one with her fists."

"And her forehead."

"And her knees."

"And elbows."

"And feet, and fingers."

"And her ax. Dinna forget the ax."

"The ax."

The flurry of words from the male dwarfs buffeted Aspen's ears and he took an involuntary step backward.

Dagmarra smiled at his stumbling, showing off all six of her teeth. "'Tis true," she said, "I'm a fine one with all that."

"Now, tell her she would've beaten you," the first dwarf said.

Aspen nodded immediately. "Bloody," he said, knowing it was true.

"You had nah chance at all," the second dwarf said.

"None whatsoever."

The two brothers looked to their sister, who shrugged. And stepped aside.

"I am Annar," the first dwarf said.

"And I am Thridi," said the second.

"And you are accepted into our *hule*."

The last bit sounded like a formal welcome, though whether he had just been accepted into their house, their kinship group, or their dinner table, Aspen was not certain, but he bowed respectfully nonetheless. "I thank you, good sirs." He turned and made another bow toward the female.

"May I ask you a question?" he began, thinking to bring up the Sticksman and perhaps find an answer to the questions he'd been geased. But before he could address her or step up and open the door to the cart, he heard hoofbeats. Lots of them.

He looked back down the road and saw a troop of mounted soldiers dressed in the livery of his father, the king. It was surely the troop that had gone by before.

Bother! he thought. *But at least Snail is safe.*

"Hold," Annar and Thridi said at the same time.

Aspen gulped. "Why do . . . don't I go on in while you . . . um . . . talk to the soldiers." The horses with their fierce-looking riders were already closer than he would have liked. *Almost close enough to see me,* he thought. *And if my brother is leading them, I* will *be taken.* His jaw was stiff. He knew he looked grim. Or frightened. Or both.

But at least they will not get Snail. He shuffled his feet impatiently. *Still, it would be better if neither of us is found out.*

"You're nah going in without me," Dagmarra said.

"And she'll nah be with you without us," Annar added.

"But . . . Nomi . . ." He found himself stumbling over Snail's false name. Said it again with a bit more authority. "Nomi went in without you." He tried not to whine, but at this point the soldiers were so close, and he could not quite keep the panic out of his voice.

"She is skarm drema," the three dwarfs said as one, as if that explained anything.

But of course, it didn't.

And now Dagmarra blocked the door and the soldiers blocked the road and Aspen was left with nothing but a lute to defend himself with. A lute with a carved and battered angel on the top of its neck, perhaps foreshadowing how Aspen would look once the soldiers caught hold of him.

Maybe, he thought, *I could hang myself quickly with the strings and save them all the trouble.*

SNAIL'S ODD ENCOUNTER

The next room was fully lit. Instead of the starkness of the caped creature's room, or the snugness of the dwarfs' room, this one looked like a place in the Unseelie palace, luxurious enough for a queen to give birth in or see ambassadors.

Snail spun around slowly, taking it in. Was this then the professor's room? All she knew of professors were that they taught dry old facts like how many Hobs could dance in a pentagram or what moon was most propitious for birth-giving or burial, or the list of the kings of the Unseelie Realm down to the fiftieth generation. Though, since her only teachers had been midwives, and professors never seemed to have babies (though how they multiplied she'd never been able to figure out), she'd never actually met one before. A professor might be as tall and thin as the Sticksman or as broad and brangling as a Border Lord. It was silly to speculate. But the room itself might hold some clues.

The one bed was enormous, with pillows of all sizes and shapes piled high and covered with cloth of silver and gold.

No one in the Unseelie world was allowed cloth of silver except a prince or princess; none allowed cloth of gold except the king or queen.

Snail drew in a quick breath. *Perhaps* . . . she thought . . . *perhaps the professor is married and needs a midwife. Perhaps that's what skarm drema meant and why I've been brought inside.* It was an interesting idea, and she considered it for a moment.

Drawing herself up, she recited the midwife creed silently, and prepared to get down to work: *Anticipate, alleviate, and then await.* She'd need hot water and soap. Wondered how that might work, given this was a wagon and they were some ways to the last stream.

She snapped her finger. Prince Aspen could say the fire charm and . . .

Stupid, she muttered, *if he did such a daft thing, he'd be giving himself away.*

She was puzzling this over when another door suddenly creaked open, this one by the right side of the bedstead. It was an ominous sound. She stood ready to flee back into the room with that annoying bird.

However, instead of something fierce coming through the door—like an ogre or troll—in glided the most beautiful woman Snail had ever seen. She was more beautiful than the twin princesses Sun and Moon, who wore their boredom on their faces, more beautiful than the Unseelie queen, who had every kind of glamour at her fingertips.

This was no professor's wife, who would undoubtedly have been a dowdy and difficult patient wanting to know all the midwifery secrets before giving birth. The woman was clearly one of the ancient Seelie goddesses. No one else could be that beautiful and serene.

Snail managed a quick and adequate curtsey, though her right knee creaked and the left one locked.

The beautiful woman glided soundlessly right up to her and held out her hand. "I am Maggie Light," she said, in a voice that was sweet without being cloying, strong without being demanding. "Not Dark. Not dark at all. Remember that."

"I will, goddess," Snail whispered to the hand.

There was a tinkling sound that Snail just managed to realize was a laugh, not bells. The proffered hand did not move away, just dangled there, as if waiting, just at Snail's sight line. At last, she realized that this Maggie Light wanted to help her up out of the curtsey.

Tentatively, Snail reached for the hand and was dragged up to her feet, like a fish caught on a hook and line.

"There, that is better," said Maggie Light.

"Better than what?" Snail muttered. But she knew. It was better than being in a dungeon or at the end of a rope. Better than being captured by one or two armies. Better than being devoured by a carnivorous merman . . .

"Now I can see your pretty face."

Pretty? Snail couldn't tell if Maggie Light always over-complimented her visitors or if she was making a joke. Or, perhaps, she was blind. Snail dared a glance at her.

Maggie Light's eyes were a strange color, a kind of silver.

And who has silver eyes, Snail thought, *except—maybe—a fish?* She tried to think of Maggie Light as a fish. A mer. She shuddered, wondering how sharp the woman's teeth were.

Almost as if reading Snail's mind, Maggie Light smiled. Her teeth were small, white, and even as pearls on a necklace. There was no threat in them. "Why have you come here, child?"

All Snail could think of to say in answer was what the dwarfs had said, the words that had worked before: "Skarm drema!"

"Ah," Maggie Light said, turning away from Snail and gliding over to a nearby desk. The desk had a slanted top and there was an open book lying there with ruled lines going both sideways and up and down.

Snail followed her and looked at the book. Things were scribbled on the page in blue and red inks.

"You are not in the diary," Maggie Light said, pointing a perfect finger at the book. "He has not put you in the diary. How unusual."

Snail shrugged. "Maybe he didn't know I was coming."

"But if you are truly skarm drema, he will know you are here."

"*I* didn't know I was here. Or even *know* I was coming here. Until I *was* here, that is," Snail said. Now that she knew she wasn't needed for a birth and she wasn't about to be eaten by an ogre or merman or troll, her irritation was beginning to show.

"Nevertheless," said Maggie Light, and then she was suddenly no longer paying attention to Snail. Instead, head cocked to one side like a bird, she stood still as stone, listening to something else. Something that Snail couldn't hear.

At last Maggie Light moved and, turning her head, announced, "He comes."

"Who? The professor?" asked Snail, adding, "And by the way, what does he profess?"

"That he will tell you himself," said Maggie Light, gliding soundlessly toward the bed as if stepping out of the way.

Out of the way of what? Snail wondered. But before she could even try to guess, the bookcase by her side swung wide and she had to scramble to avoid being hit. It was a third door into the room. *Is three the charm?*

A figure strode through.

Snail had been expecting someone taller. Someone fiercer. Someone . . . consequential.

The man who came through the door was small and round, a gourd of a man, with thinning hair, a short grey goatee, and twinkly grey eyes. *Grey.* No one in the Seelie Courts had grey eyes. Unless . . . unless perhaps they were related to fish. She wondered if it was a coincidence that both the professor and Maggie Light had grey eyes. Father and daughter? Uncle and niece? Some other family connection she wasn't acquainted with?

"Hello," the man said in a voice like bubbling water. "Nice to have you here, *here* being the operative word. At least the way we operate."

"Operate? Are you a doctor then?" Snail asked.

"I can strike a set but not set a leg," he told her. "I can boil a lance but not lance a boil. I . . ."

Decidedly not a fish, Snail thought. Fish folk rarely spoke above water, or so she'd heard. The one mer she'd had a close encounter with had said nothing.

". . . I'm Professor Odds," he said, before adding, "Odds are you weren't expecting someone like me."

In a day of strangeness, he was perhaps the oddest thing of all.

6

ASPEN'S LOUTISH CAST

*A*spen pulled off his lute and fervently wished for his lost hat to hide his face. As he did so, he remembered his speech to Snail about the "hooded face" and the "concealing cloak."

Brave words, he thought, *but putting them to practice is proving harder than I thought.* He peered at the oncoming horsemen, trying to see if he recognized any of them. Or if any of them seemed to recognize him. He thought of swinging his lute like a weapon to hold off the soldiers, but quickly realized how useless that would be.

The incoming riders were only a small company, but a company nonetheless and plenty big enough to capture a single princeling and a midwife's apprentice.

Maybe if I surrender quietly, they won't look for Snail. For some reason this was the thought that calmed him. He nodded to himself. *If I cannot win, at least I can lose with dignity.*

He caught Annar looking at him and then at the approaching soldiers. Then the dwarf exchanged a quick glance with his brother. Aspen thought something wordless passed between them. He had no idea what and had no time to ask. The soldiers were nearly upon them.

"Tune it," Thridi said to Aspen, pointing at the lute.

Aspen was surprised but did as Thridi asked, as the two brothers stepped out in front of the first pair of trotting horses.

"Hello and be welcome!" Annar hailed them.

"Be welcome and hello!" Thridi called.

Aspen stared over the dwarfs' heads at the officers at the front of the column. He didn't recognize either of them. *But surely they have a description of me. One good look and . . .*

He heard a loud, sharp whistle and then the sound of a door slamming. As he started to turn toward the sound, a low hiss interrupted his thoughts.

"Tune it louder, foolish popinjay, and dinna look backward, never backward," Dagmarra whispered, stepping in front of him.

He saw something white stuffed into her ears but had little time to wonder at it.

"Welcome, hello, and be!" Dagmarra shouted while each of the three siblings dropped into a low bow.

Which from a dwarf, Aspen thought wildly, *is very low indeed.*

"Tune!" Dagmarra said again, hissing as if in a whisper, though it was hardly that. More of a hushed shout, as if she had no idea how loud her voice was. "And dinna make it soft."

Aspen continued to tune his lute, all the while keeping an eye on the coming soldiers.

The officer in charge, a captain by the stripes on his left shoulder, kicked his horse forward a step. His long ears marked him as old for his job, though his face was relatively unlined. Judging by the frayed coat he wore, the single battle medal on his chest, and the small number of soldiers he commanded, Aspen thought the captain was probably not from a good family or otherwise well connected.

The captain looked down his long nose at the strange tableau before him and wrinkled his brow. "Well met, Little Folk," he said, nodding his head at the bowing dwarfs. Then he turned his gaze to Aspen. "And . . . minstrel?"

The captain's eyes bored into his, and Aspen was sure he was about to be called out. Though he didn't recognize the officer, by the way the captain was staring, he surely suspected something.

He knows it is me, Aspen thought. *He is only playing games now, waiting for me to confess.* Aspen set his feet in a wider stance to keep from trembling, and straightened his shoulders. *Well, I shall not confess. If I am to be captured, it will not be by my own admission. And I will give this petty tyrant— this underthing, this nobody—no enjoyment of the . . .*

Suddenly, Aspen was bent over at the waist and struggling for a breath. Dagmarra's face was level with his own and he smelled the rotten-gums stench of her breath. It took a moment for him to realize she had just turned and punched him in the stomach. Hard! How she missed destroying the lute with the blow he could not figure out.

"Bow down to your betters, you scurvy music maker," she said, rather loudly into his face, her perilous breath wafting even farther into his own mouth. Loud enough, he was sure, for the whole troop to hear and laugh at him.

But better, he thought, *to be laughed at that than dangle at the end of a rope. Though*—and of this he was certain—*certainly not as noble.*

"Yes," Annar said pleasantly to the captain, "that is our minstrel."

"A talented musician," Thridi added. "Though a bit touched in the head."

"Thick as soup," said Annar. "If truth be told."

"Doesn't even know to bow to his betters," said Thridi.

"Forgets to eat."

"Like to starve if we don't look after him."

"Dense as stone."

"Slow as snails."

"Dull as dust."

"Dim-witted, you could say," Dagmarra added.

Aspen felt they had made their point three or four metaphors earlier, but he wasn't going to complain. Instead he straightened up but no longer preened like a prince. Rather, he looked down at his lute and started tuning it again, this time softly, all the while managing to keep a watch on things out of the corner of his right eye.

Dagmarra grinned gap-toothed up at the captain and stroked her beard.

The officer finally looked away and nodded to the other officer, a lieutenant by his stripes. The lieutenant was a much younger elf wearing a better cut of uniform. His hair had a green stripe on either side, marking him as a recruit and lower class at that, though to have become an officer meant he had done the crown some other service.

Possibly spying, Aspen thought. *Possibly a member of the Assassins' Guild. Even the Seelie Court had such a thing*, or so his tutor Jaunty had taught him. The difference between the Unseelie assassins and the Seelie were the ways in which they killed. Aspen thought briefly of the two who had been ready to finish him off in the Unseelie dungeon, the ones he evaded more by accident than design. He shook his head. *This Seelie lieutenant looks nothing like them.* They had been coarse boggarts after all, not elves.

The lieutenant pulled a scroll from his saddlebag and handed it to the captain, looking at once both eager to do the captain's bidding and annoyed.

"Well," the captain said, glancing down at the scroll before continuing in stentorian tones. "I am searching for Prince Ailenbran Astaeri and a companion. They are wanted by the King's Justice, and all in the realm must assist in their discoverance."

Aspen waited for the dwarfs to name him and braced himself to run, forgetting for a moment his plan to retain his dignity.

But Annar just cocked his head to one side and said, "We've seen nah soul who gave us that name."

The captain nodded. "He has most likely taken an alias."

"Ah," Annar said, nodding back as if in appreciation of the captain's wisdom.

"What alias is he using then?" Thridi asked. He wasn't nodding.

"We do not know," the captain said.

"Then why tell us his name?" Annar stopped nodding and scratched his chin beneath his long beard.

"When it could be any?" Thridi added.

"Might as well ask for Robert the Woodcutter."

"Or James of the Loch."

"Or Pitter Pat Pettenby the Poor Peddler of Pottery."

"Or perhaps ask for our sister, Dagmarra here."

The captain stared at Dagmarra and especially at her beard. His pale skin turned even paler.

"Best not," Annar said.

"Doubt ye could handle her," Thridi concluded.

"Well . . . I . . ." the captain stammered, which made the lieutenant hide a smile behind his hand. The captain's horse stomped the ground as if echoing its rider's discomfort.

Aspen kept on tuning, even though the notes were not getting any better.

"Perhaps you could tell us what this offender looks like?" Annar suggested.

"Give us the lay of the land, so to speak," Thridi said.

"If the land were his face," Annar said by way of explanation.

"And your kind words the map," concluded Thridi.

"Well," the captain said, glancing between the dwarf brothers momentarily before giving his head a quick shake and looking down at the scroll. "Golden hair," he read. "And a bit short for a royal." He looked up from the scroll and pointed at Aspen.

Shocked, Aspen accidentally tweaked the lute's second string hard. The noise was that of a cracked bell crossed with a bowstring snapping, and the dwarfs and the officers all cringed.

When the last sound of the twanged string faded, the captain said, "From the description here, he bears a fair resemblance to your minstrel there. What is his name?"

"Karl," Aspen said at the same time that Dagmarra said, "Popinjay."

"Karl Popinjay," Annar said smoothly.

"A *more* than fair resemblance," the captain said, then sighed. "But without the loutish cast to the features or the dim look in the eyes." He leaned forward and patted his horse on the neck. "I imagine being a prince, he would be unable to hide his royal bearing."

The dwarfs nodded in agreement as Aspen thought, *Loutish cast? Dim look in my eyes?*

"You have not seen him, then?" the captain asked.

"No princes," Annar said.

"Nor companions," Thridi said.

The lieutenant and his horse moved closer to the captain, and the lieutenant whispered in the captain's ear. The captain nodded carefully, then said loudly, "Call the dismount!"

The lieutenant whistled back to the troops, who immediately dismounted in unison, the sound of two dozen boots hitting the ground at once like a kettle drum in the morning air.

Then the captain dismounted smoothly and silently and handed his reins to Annar, who was suddenly by his side. "We have not yet broken our fast this morning, dwarf. Have your Popinjay warble for us whilst we eat."

"Of course!" Annar said enthusiastically. He turned to Aspen. "Karl? Are you in tune?"

Aspen tried to remain calm, but his thoughts were racing. *What can I do? I can play, but cannot sing. The officer's horse likely has a better voice than me! And if I cannot sing, will I be unmasked as a minstrel? And if I am not a minstrel, will they see that maybe my features aren't so loutish, my eyes not so dim, my bearing a mite more princely than peasantly?*

"Karl?" Thridi said.

"Popinjay?" Annar said.

"My . . . um . . ." Aspen stuttered. "My singer . . ."

"Is Maggie Light," Dagmarra said. "I'll go fetch her. Perhaps an instrumental till she arrives?"

Aspen looked at Dagmarra gratefully. At that moment no princess so fair could have looked more beautiful to him than the gap-toothed, bearded dwarf female who had been ready to pound him into the ground just a few moments earlier.

Thank you, he mouthed at her, wondering who Maggie Light was, hoping it would not be Snail in disguise. Then he turned back to the soldiers, who were digging in their packs for waybread and water. And, after sliding the second string back into key, he launched into the old Seelie air called "The Loves of Leannan Sidhe," pleased that he was only slightly out of tune and hoping no one else would notice.

SNAIL PEEPS

$\mathcal{S}$nail was about to introduce herself when there was a sharp whistle that seemed to pierce the room. In the next room the bird started to squawk, "Pay the troll, pay the troll!" and the rug thing with the teeth bounded, or rather slid, into the room. Both the professor and Maggie Light startled like hares, their heads turned simultaneously not to the bird or the incoming floor creature, but toward the bookcase door. It was as if they were both hearing something else, something that Snail couldn't hear.

"What?" Snail asked.

Turning to glance at her, the professor scowled, then turned again to the bookcase door.

This time Snail heard what they heard: the thump of booted feet hitting the ground in unison. It was loud and imposing and unmistakable: soldiers dismounting.

She knew such a sound, often hearing it when the Unseelie soldiers had done their morning maneuvers beyond the castle walls—the multiple boots striking the ground at the same time, accompanied by the drum cadencing the count for the men.

This time there was no drum, no drummer, but this sound was terrible and upsetting because Aspen was outside. *Outside with a company of soldiers.* That did not bode well. *He is incapable of pretending*, she thought. *The soldiers are sure to figure out he's a prince the minute he opens his mouth. Or straightens his shoulders. Or gives one of them a withering toff look.* She knew in fact that he was nobly stupid enough to turn himself in to save her.

"Sir!" she said to the professor, ready to confess all if he would just use his magic to save Aspen. "Sir, please . . ."

Hissssst! Maggie Light had one beautiful finger pressed firmly against her beautiful lips and was making a sound like a serpent.

In that instant, as if by magic, Snail was silenced. She opened her mouth to beg again and nothing came out.

Meanwhile the professor was again doing something odd. He'd turned and pressed his face against the wall, which had a painted surface of red and gold flowers. His shoulder was right next to the bookcase. And there he stood for a long moment. When at last he turned and looked back, he said to Maggie Light, "The performance of your life, girl. You're performing *for* a life. You were made for this. Make it work. Now!"

She nodded and went out the door she'd first come in.

"As for you, young woman," Professor Odds said to Snail,

his silver eyes boring into hers, "stay safe in here. If you must know what's unfolding, the wall will tell you." Then he went around the bookcase, to the door space, and the bookcase closed behind him.

Odder and odder, Snail thought, though oddest of all, she didn't disobey him. Instead, trusting the professor, trusting his magic, she went at once to the wall.

Standing where he'd stood, Snail pressed close to the wall.

"All right, wall," she whispered, feeling foolish, "unfold." She leaned forward until her nose touched it, and suddenly the center of one of the red painted flowers resolved into a peephole.

A peephole!

That was a bit disappointing as it wasn't magic at all. But nevertheless, she looked through and realized she could see soldiers standing by their horses, a captain and his lieutenant conferring, the three dwarfs, and best of all, Prince Aspen—so far unharmed—playing the lute. *Badly*, she supposed. She realized rather late that she couldn't hear the lute, or anything else for that matter.

As the dumb show unfolded, Snail watched as Professor Odds came out to greet the soldiers, arms wide, like a small ringmaster of a tiny traveling circus.

The men all turned to him, the lieutenant looking a bit amused and a lot suspicious; the captain, his face souring, obviously annoyed. The three dwarfs she couldn't read because their backs were turned to her, though they seemed to be fiddling with their ears. But at least they stood at attention, more so than the soldiers. She was pleased about that. She'd bet those three dwarfs against that ragtag soldiery any day.

And Aspen? He kept doggedly playing his tune, whatever it was.

Snail sighed. The professor had said the wall would tell her. And so it had, in a limited way. But she wanted to know more, not just sit hidden in the cart, only guessing at what was being said. She'd just about decided she had to go outside, when—*suddenly*—everything changed.

Maggie Light's voice came soaring over the landscape, and oddly enough, Snail could hear it even through the walls of the cart, though the walls had probably strained out most of its power. Maggie Light was singing the words to an old tune, one Snail could sort of remember and almost name.

> The gate between the trees is open.
> The way will be quite steep.
> Stones as hard as hearts the markers.
> Do not weep, child, do not weep.

Her voice was as clear as glass, as sharp as a knife, as comforting as a lullaby. The soldiers seemed stunned, mouths open. The captain had begun to drool. The lieutenant tried to struggle a bit against the magic; got one finger up to his ear, before he, too, went slack-jawed.

Without going under, you can't get through.
You are the path that has been made.
Leaves can tremble without falling,
Shadows cast can still give shade.

Aspen's fingers had fallen from the strings. He, too, was charmed, mazed.

Only the dwarfs and the professor seemed untouched by the song. And Snail, somehow secure inside the cart, was untouched as well, the walls having kept her safe from the spell.

One foot, then, and now the next one,
Forward, downward, going deep.
Turn over stones, remark the Under.
Do not weep, child, do not weep.

The professor walked over to the lieutenant and then the captain, whispering in their ears. Then he came back to Aspen and put a hand on his shoulder, spun him around, caught the lute when it started to drop from the prince's flaccid fingers. Then he walked Aspen, all unresisting, up the stairs and into the cart.

Maggie Light's song stopped.

The dwarfs took out whatever had been stuffed into their ears.

The captain and lieutenant looked around as if wondering

what they were doing there. Then they signaled to the soldiers to remount, got back on their horses themselves, and rode off.

As a show, Snail thought, it had everything—good characters, tense action, and a happy ending.

But as real life—well, she thought, *it's very odd indeed.*

ASPEN AWAKENS

She was beautiful. A silver goddess with a voice of gold. She didn't ask what tune Aspen was playing, and he'd never before heard the lyrics she sang. Had not even known the song had lyrics. But somehow they fit. No, they more than fit. They meshed. They melded. They grew into something greater than a song. Something that enraptured and captured and . . .

"Put me to sleep?" Aspen came to himself with a start. It must have all been a dream. He lay on a large, soft bed, richly surrounded by silken pillows of gold and silver.

I don't remember any goddess! he thought desperately, sitting up. *I don't remember this bed. This place. How long have I been dreaming?*

Then he realized that he must be inside the players' wagon, the very place he had been trying to get to when everything had fallen apart.

The wagon! The soldiers!

That's when he had an additional thought: *How far have we traveled?*

He looked for a window to check the rate of their speed and saw a large one, which was very strange to him because castle windows are always mere arrow slits, built that way in case of an assault. This window overlooked a field of stunning flowers, and even stranger, they were not moving.

I don't remember fields of flowers, he thought, still drowsy. And then he had a further thought: *The wagon must be as becalmed as a sailing ship on a breezeless ocean.*

He had never sailed on the ocean, though he had a vague memory of watching from a cliff-top far north of Astaeri Palace as a two-masted boat with an oddly round body headed for the northern islands. It was winter and his tiny hand clasped in his mother's firm grip was the only part of him that felt warm and protected from the cold, whipping wind.

His only other ocean memory was from a song. He began to sing it to himself, trying to recall where he'd heard it.

> The water is wide, my dear,
> The water is deep.
> The strand is long, my dear,
> But love will keep . . .

When he had first heard the song, he must have already lived a year in the Unseelie Court, still mourning the loss of his own family. A minstrel had performed for King Obs, a minstrel who had a strange wandering eye. The Border

Lords had thrown bones at him and called him misfigured, but Aspen had thought the song pretty and sad at the same time, though he had only understood a small part of it. He felt terrible for the minstrel, who was clearly as out of place at the Unseelie Court as Aspen was. Jaunty had had to explain to him that the song was about the ocean and that a strand was a fancy Unseelie word for a beach.

Suddenly, he realized that there really *was* no breeze outside. It took him a minute more to realize that the flowers were part of a painting, a clever trompe l'oeil that depicted a window looking out onto a pasture full of blooming poppies.

Someone nearby cleared his throat.

Aspen turned his head. The three dwarfs stood by the far wall across from the flower painting, their beards almost hiding the concern in their faces. Plumping a pillow behind him was the stunning woman from his dream, who leaned closer as if to examine him. His heart stuttered in his chest and he looked away. Inside, he was repeating over and over, She is real! She is real!

There was a grey-eyed manservant hulking in the shadows behind her, probably a clerk by his manner and dress.

Finally, nearest to the bed and looking down at him, her mismatched eyes sparkling with anger or amusement or relief—maybe all three at once—was Snail.

"Hello," he said, shooting her a weak smile. She nodded and he tried to guess whether they were in trouble.

Are we captured? Are we among friends? What happened outside? He did not know which question to ask first, and anyway he certainly did not want to appear panicked in front of the beautiful singer, so instead he tried to sound nonchalant, casual, smooth. "I played a song."

More slow than smooth, Your Serenity, he thought. *Are you trying to live up to the dwarfs' description of you?* That much he remembered! *Dull as dust and dense as stone?*

But Snail's face broke into a pleasant grin and she answered him as if he had dispensed the deepest of wisdoms. "Yes, Karl. You did."

For a moment he could not remember who Karl was, but when he recalled that was his minstrel name, he smiled back.

"And the song was beautiful," added the stunning woman. "It felt right for me to fit the words to your tune."

Her words? My tune? That was when Aspen fully realized that the dream was not a dream but something that had really happened. *Unless, of course, I am still asleep and dreaming.*

Surreptitiously, he pinched his left pointer finger. It hurt. So—he was awake!

Maggie Light, he thought suddenly. He was pleased he remembered her name.

Clambering off the bed, he gave Maggie Light a deep, courtly bow, though his legs were wobbly. "It was a bare collection of notes before you gave it wings." He knew Snail would say he sounded like a toff, but there was no way to express his amazement at Maggie's singing in a commoner's plain speaking. "Your voice is . . . transcendent."

The manservant spoke then. "Even magical, you might say."

Aspen shook his head. He was born and bred to magic and had sensed no glamour while she sang. And besides . . . "How would you know magic, mud-man. You are a—"

"Yes," the manservant interrupted in a stern voice that somehow stopped Aspen cold.

Belatedly, Aspen realized that traveling minstrels—unlike royalty—must have to deal with all species of peoples on a relatively even footing. And if those people had just saved his life, the footing was probably considerably *less* than even.

"I . . . um . . . apologize," he stuttered, unsure of how to do it formally without sounding too toffly. "I have forgotten my manners. And—"

"And you're unused to dealing with my people as, well, people," the manservant said, interrupting Aspen again. "Everyone to you is an animal or a manimal." He held Aspen's gaze with his steel-grey eyes, daring him to contradict the statement. Aspen felt that the man was judging him, marking his pros and cons in a mental clerk's ledger. He did not think the man was wasting a lot of ink in the "pros" column.

"Um . . . yes . . . look . . . I . . ." Aspen sighed. He really didn't want to apologize to the clerk again. But he did not want to offend the touchy creature, either. Or make the stunning Maggie Light think less of him. "Perhaps, if I could just talk to your master, and thank him for his assistance, we could . . ." He trailed off as the clerk looked at him as if he were Dagmarra's spit drying in the dust outside the wagon.

Shaking his head, the clerk turned to the dwarfs. "Dagmarra. Boys. Let's get moving before the soldiers remember where they were going. And do what they remember they were planning to do."

The dwarfs nodded and shuttled out. Thridi was last through the door, and Aspen thought he heard him mutter, "Dim-witted, you might say."

The clerk then looked at Snail. "When you are done greeting your *minstrel,* your *wastrel,* perhaps we could have a word alone?" To Maggie he practically snarled, "I don't want to see him again."

"Yes, Professor," she said to his back as he stomped out of the room, making the sound of soldiers leading a man to his execution.

Aspen gaped at the door through which the dwarfs and the clerk had just exited. Then he looked at Maggie, who was frowning. It did not make her any less beautiful. Only then did he turn to Snail, who was glaring at him.

"Professor?" he said. "*That's* Professor Odds?"

"Yes," Snail said grimly, "and odds are you weren't expecting someone like him." She followed the professor out the door.

"I'm sorry," Aspen said to no one in particular.

Maggie Light gave a soft giggle that burbled like a mountain brook. "Not yet you aren't, but I imagine you will be soon. He can do that to people." She put a light hand on his shoulder. "Come, let's find you somewhere to stay, Popinjay. *This* room is already taken."

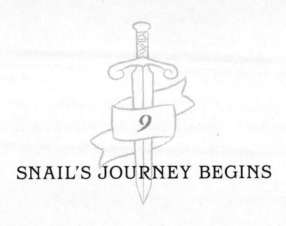

SNAIL'S JOURNEY BEGINS

The professor slumped into a chair by a workbench in the small room. To the side of the workbench was a single bed, its covers pulled so tight, they almost seemed painted on.

The workbench itself was covered with small silvery beads and strands of wire. There were silver implements like nothing Snail had ever seen: odd pincers with tiny pointed ends, hefty scissors that looked as if they could shear through cold iron, and three sizes of hammers, each smaller than the last. A pair of very strange glasses lay to one side, with lenses as thick as winter ice.

Snail thought the professor might be a crafter who made jewelry to sell at their performances, not a magician at all. She'd seen no jewels on either the dwarf woman or Maggie Light, but that could mean nothing. *After all, midwives don't deliver their own babies.* How often had Mistress Softhands said so.

But, she told herself, some of those tools might be useful for midwives. She glanced again at the scissors, saw a small pair in silver that might be just the thing. And a pair of silver tongs small enough to fit this task. She wondered if she might ask the professor to borrow them in case . . .

Then she had to laugh at herself. Tongs. Just what a midwife always needs. But these are much too tiny to fit around a baby's head, whether elf or brownie. Besides, who would be giving birth here—*Maggie Light? The dwarf woman? Besides, I don't wish to reveal who I really am.*

But, in fact, all the new tools were tempting. Her fingers itched to try each one.

"That *friend* of yours!" Professor Odds's voice dripped with sarcasm that slashed through her reverie. "That so-called Karl . . ."

"Just Karl, sir. Not So-called Karl," Snail said, trying to make light of it. Hoping she was succeeding.

"Do you think a professor is fooled by such a Karl-less name? I'm trained to identify such improbables. I have degrees in it. I would take odds against it. In fact, as Odds, I *am* against it."

Snail's head was spinning. She couldn't tell if he was speaking sense or nonsense. Or both at once.

Hardly noticing her response, the professor continued. "He is no doubt called Prince Balersterei Meddlesome IV, or some such nonsense. Karl does not suit him. The plainness of it. The short, sharp shock of it. He should be wearing a high-sounding name and a high-fashion suit. Not the way he talks, all hoity and toity, all furbelows, falsettos, and false-set-tos. And tiresome beyond measure." He rubbed his right eye.

"He's not like that at all," Snail said, though she knew that sometimes he was. But they'd rescued each other so often, she and Aspen, that defending him was the very least she could do.

"I have performed for and dined with his kind for years now," Odds said, his voice harsh with the criticism. "It never gets easier. They all think that who they were born to gives them the right to . . ."

Snail had to stop herself from shuddering. Such talk could get them all imprisoned, or put to the flames. She tried again, keeping her tone mild. "That is not how I know him, sir. And he thinks his rank . . ." She bit her lips and added hastily, "Whatever that rank is . . . that it means he has to act nobly."

The professor's lips drew together as if he'd suddenly tasted a sour piece of fruit. "Don't keep addressing me as *sir*, child. Professor will do nicely, thank you. After all, it's *my* rank. And I got it the hard way." He smiled slyly. "I earned it!"

"Professor," said Snail, but she spoke it the way people at the Unseelie Court did, with a certain amount of casual disdain that was not lost on Odds at all, "I think you are mistaking Karl."

He smiled slowly, as if deliberately ignoring her small insolence, and said, "Then there is a huge gap, a crevasse, a cavern between how he thinks he should act and how he actually does."

Snail wasn't sure what he was talking about. *Crevasse* was not a word she'd ever heard before. But she could tell from his tone what he meant. "He was the Hos—" she began, and then paused. Wouldn't it be better to keep that information to herself? Or should she just trust the professor, despite his remarks about Prince Aspen? About toffs in general? After all, except for Aspen she felt the same way about them. And Odds *had* magicked the two of them away from the soldiers. With Maggie Light's help, of course. Surely he meant no harm to the prince or to her.

But suddenly her mind whirled with alternatives: The professor could be waiting to sell them both to the highest bidder. He could want to turn them in to the king himself on his own terms, maybe get himself a higher rank by doing so. *He could be willing to bide his time and wreak vengeance on both courts—since clearly he doesn't like toffs. He could use Aspen to . . . to . . .* Here her imagination stopped working and she ran out of possibilities.

That was when she realized this strange man was in fact truly strange, an actual *stranger* to them. She'd no idea *what* he thought or *how* he thought. But since, all her life, everything she'd ever heard about the Seelie folk was how twisty and untrustworthy they were, in the end she thought it was best to say nothing at all.

Odds turned his steely eyes on her. "Karl was *what?*" he asked, his voice low, soothing.

She didn't dare keep looking at those steel-colored eyes. She'd already seen the things he could do with them. Instead she hastily glanced down at the floor. "He was the host— the host—of a rival troop of soldiers at his . . . um . . . great hall and things went badly. So the other soldiers are looking to punish him. Us. Thank you for helping." She didn't dare let him see the lies fully exposed in her eyes, in the hot flush on her cheeks. She was not practiced in lying.

"Always a pleasure, if a measured one," mumbled the professor, "not quite a quart but more than a cup." He turned away as if he didn't believe her or else really didn't care. But as long as Odds was hiding them from harm—at least from *some* harm—she thought she should try and be nice to him.

"Those are very interesting tools," she said, changing the subject. It was an awkward shift and she was sure he had known at once what she was trying to do, but she kept at it anyway, pointing to several hammers and a clamp, but never at the ones she had a real interest in, for fear of giving herself away completely.

"You like tools?" he asked quickly.

That surprised her, and then she thought, *He spoke* too *quickly.*

"I . . . I liked to watch the cook boys polishing the master chef's knives and forks and things," she said, "when we were fed after a performance." *That was smooth*, she thought, and warming to her story, she added, "My. . . um . . . da was a . . . a . . ." her mind went blank for a moment trying to conjure up this pretend father and then she had it. "The town blacksmith. And he had a lot of . . . um . . . tools, too. Smithing tools." She took a deep breath, knowing that while she'd started well enough, things were now going badly. "And my mam, well she was a midwife." She could tell him that without saying she herself was a midwife's apprentice and still be on firmer ground. "And Mam, she had lovely tools. Small hand tongs for the breach babes, and soft linen ropes to help pull out a tardy infant, and silver scissors like those there . . ." she pointed to the professor's table. She saw he was staring intently at her face and, blushing, she finished with a rush. "But I didn't want to be a blacksmith or a birther so I ran away to the city to join a troop of roaming players and there . . ."

"There you met our toff, who decided to take you with him on the road," Odds said. "A pretty enough story if it were true. But . . ."

And just as he was going to uncover her true occupation— she was sure of it—the floor gave a sudden jolt, the walls began to creak ominously, and Snail almost lost her footing.

"Ah," said Professor Odds, raising his right hand with the pointing finger straight up and the other fingers curled. "We have begun." He pronounced the words like a wizard's incantation, and at that, the players' long cart started to move.

Snail glanced around for a window to see exactly where

they were going, but there was none. Not even an arrow slit. *Perhaps another peephole?* If there was one here, she couldn't identify it. *Besides, I can't just walk up to the wall and search for one, can I? I can't be that obvious.*

"What *have* we begun, professor?" she asked, hoping it sounded innocent and not desperate.

"We have begun the beginning of your journey and the end of mine; the first step of many and the last step of even more. Our journey home," he said.

Home? It was the last place in the world she wanted to go. All that awaited her there was a dungeon and death. But how could she tell him that?

From what he'd said so far, she'd have laid odds herself that he didn't care what she thought at all.

❖ ❖ ❖

THE DOOR OF the professor's room opened and Maggie Light came through, gliding in that unforced way that continued to astonish Snail.

"I have put the boy in with the twins," she told the professor. "The bowser is already complaining. It is past time, I think, to give it a bath and brush its teeth."

"Let *Karl* do that when we stop for the night," said the professor, emphasizing the prince's new name with such disdain, Snail knew he wasn't going to let the matter go.

"I'll gladly do it," said Snail quickly, happy to have something else to talk about. "In my . . . um . . . profession, we know how to clean things." And then she realized she'd given away half of what she'd already told him. He would guess now that she was, like her make-believe mother, a birther after all.

"A bowser," the professor said dryly, as if he'd noticed nothing, "is not a thing but rather an animate rug. It herds *things*. And this one is not fond of females. Best leave it to the *host*." He emphasized the last word, which made Snail understand that he hadn't been fooled for even an instant by what she'd considered her quick thinking.

I am such *a bad liar*, she thought. *Besides, I can always help the prince bathe the bowser when no one is paying us any attention.*

It was the last thought she had before the cart began to shudder and shake so badly, it was as if the road had suddenly developed contractions and was about to give birth.

ASPEN HOBBLES A UNICORN

*A*spen sat in the drab room Maggie Light had led him to and moped.

Has it really come to this? He looked at the grey cloaks hanging from the walls, the dull brown rug, the bed he assumed he'd have to share with the room's other occupants. *At least at the Unseelie castle he'd had his own room.*

Fallen! he thought miserably. He had to take a deep breath in order not to cry.

Lying down on the smallest of the single beds, he stared at the ceiling, willing this to be a nightmare from which he could wake up. He never noticed the wagon had started to move. He was already asleep when the rocking began.

He awakened with a start some time later. He was never to know how long he had been out. But the bed was swaying. The entire room was swaying, and not in a good way. He could feel his stomach becoming more and more upset. Sitting up, he was glad that he had had no lunch, or the rug would have ended up even more discolored in the very near future.

When the wagon finally found a smooth part of the road, Aspen lay back down on the bed, but as soon as he did, the room twirled and swirled and his belly rumbled and . . .

He jumped to his feet and swallowed forcefully, commanding his innards to behave.

They listened.

For now.

A sudden shuddering and juddering of the wagon began with a single bounce that almost sent him sprawling on the floor. It went on for some time. Soon the wagon was regularly alternating between a smooth ride and a jouncy one.

It was amazing to him that nothing had fallen off shelves and onto the floor until he realized that everything in the room was tied down in one way or another: brushes and water cups and clothing were all packed securely in boxes that were tacked to the sides of the wagon.

Just as he made this discovery, the wagon began to shudder more violently than before. He thought he was going to be forced to decide between being sick on the rug or finding a door or window to fling himself out of, when as suddenly as the shaking had begun, it stopped.

With a great sigh of relief, Aspen threw himself instead back onto the bed. But before he could even close his eyes, Maggie Light returned.

"Dear Karl," she said sweetly, tossing some odd implements onto the bed next to him. "We have found our place for the night. You're to hobble the unicorns and gather wood for a fire."

"Me?" Aspen asked. "Surely you have . . ." *Servants for that?* he stopped himself from saying. *They're all barely more than servants themselves. This really is going to take a lot of getting used to.* "Someone more experienced in doing that?" he finished lamely.

"Oh, it's just like hobbling a horse," Maggie said, as if everyone knew how to do *that*. "The unicorns are well trained. You should have no problem."

Surely, he thought, *she is joking.* He tried to smile and failed.

"Well, then I shall have to try." He meant it to sound jolly, cooperative, but even he could see it was tentative and graceless. Begrudging, even. As if he didn't really think it was a joke. Or did not enjoy jokes. Or . . .

And then he looked at what she'd thrown onto the bed: leather cuffs, connected in pairs by a short, thick rope. Four sets in all. If it *was* a joke, it was a very carefully thought through, elaborate jest indeed.

But something niggled at the back of his mind. He realized it was the thing he had tried to speak before. The question from the Sticksman. He opened his mouth to ask, but Maggie Light shook her head.

"You must get it done. The professor requires it." It was

as if her voice laid an enchantment over him, stronger than the geas, if such was possible.

He sighed. "I'll just go do that, then. I mean now."

Maggie Light chuckled at his discomfort and left.

With another, even greater sigh, Aspen gathered up the hobbles and followed.

❖ ❖ ❖

Outside, the setting sun was just approaching the horizon and light the color of honey slanted across the landscape.

The wagon had been pulled off the road into a wooded glade that Aspen had to admit was quite beautiful. A stream ran past a stand of fruiting thorn bushes, and tall pines were scattered about, their needles coating the ground. A copse of pine kept the land below clear of undergrowth and would mean, he assumed, fewer bothersome animals at night.

One large pine had fallen, evidently years ago, though its large root system still lay exposed to the elements, looking like some kind of instrument of torture.

So much for beauty, Aspen thought.

Snail and Odds sat on the smallest section of the tree's trunk, deep in conversation.

Aspen gave himself a brief moment of wishing he was in the professor's place, sitting comfortably and talking idly, but he had been given servant's work to do. *And I must be about it*, he thought, *earn my keep, even though I keep no earnings from the task.*

The dwarfs were just pulling the unicorns from their traces, leaping acrobatically onto one another's shoulders to reach them.

They nodded at the hobbles Aspen held. He wondered if he should hand them over to the dwarfs but, as he approached, they walked away from the unicorns without a word.

Free of their bindings, the unicorns clomped directly over to the thorn bushes and began munching away.

So, Aspen thought miserably, *now I must hobble those horned beasts. I wonder why, as they seem perfectly contented to stay and eat. Why should they wander off anyway?* He shook his head. *Longing for freedom?* He doubted they had ever been free. *Bred in captivity, more likely.* Then what? *So they are comfortable and have little fear?* None but an ogre could possibly be a match for them. *And there are no such creatures hereabouts. They are Unseelie folk.*

He shuddered, his body telling him what his mind had refused to consider: If war was truly come to the Seelie kingdom, ogres and Red Caps and Border Lords in their wild hunt would make quick work of such tamed unicorns, hobbled or not. *Better to let them run free,* he thought. *At least that way they might have a chance . . . Hobbled, they had none at all.*

But no—he had orders to hobble them and so he must. Karl would do it, even if Prince Aspen would not.

He approached the creatures with caution. They were huge, after all, and he was barely able to see over their backs.

Eighteen hands at the shoulder? Twenty? He was proud of himself for remembering how to measure horses, but he hadn't ridden one since he was seven and still lived at Astaeri Palace in the Seelie Court. And at that age, of course, he had only been allowed to ride ponies.

They do not ride horses at the Unseelie castle, he thought bitterly. *They eat them.*

Aspen looked down at the hobbles in his hand. Obviously the cuffs went around the unicorns' ankles—if ankles they were called. *Riders had odd names for the parts of their mounts,* he thought. For all he knew, unicorn ankles were called *joists* or *bounders* or *skarm drema.* He would have to ask the dwarfs, but in a way that did not make him sound dim-witted or moon-touched. But of course the hobbles had to fit there, around the ankles, whatever they were called, because the hobbles obviously would not fit around anything else except their horns, and he wasn't about to go near those. Besides, even a novice unicorn handler—as he surely was—could see *that* wasn't the way to hobble them.

But *which* ankles? *Front or rear?* He tried to remember what the servants had done back when he had been a child, but in his experience, you simply got off your mount and threw your reins to a servant when you were done riding. And that was that.

So, if I do not know by experience, I must use logic.

He looked at the unicorns, then back at the hobbles again, trying to imagine the two going together. The rope wasn't long enough to go from front leg to back leg, so he pictured the hobbles on a unicorn's front legs first. Then he made the unicorn in his mind try to walk with them on. The beast stumbled and fell forward, its horn sticking comically into the ground. He tried imagining them on the back ankles, then, and his mental unicorn stumbled, but only dragged its hind legs without falling.

"The back legs it is, then," he said with more confidence than he felt.

Approaching the unicorns cautiously, he made the kind of cooing sounds he thought an ostler would use when approaching strange animals.

One of the unicorns looked back at him suspiciously, but the other three kept munching on berries.

Aspen held one hand up in what he hoped was a reassuring gesture, and kept the other—the one with the hobbles—behind his back. He decided to approach the unicorn that was already staring at him.

At least I won't surprise him.

"There, there," he said to his target. "I am just going to make you lot safer for the evening."

To Aspen's untrained eye, the unicorn seemed calm enough, and when he was within arm's reach, he gave it a pat on its right haunch.

"There, there," he said again, and the beast turned its head back to the bushes.

Crouching down, Aspen placed all but one of the set of

hobbles on the ground and squatted at the unicorn's right rear leg. Only then did he realize he should have looked more carefully at how the cuffs worked before he was practically underneath the animal.

Well, he thought, *I am here now and they look simple enough: wrap it around the leg and fasten the dual buckles as if attaching pieces of armor, or a belt.*

Initially things went smoothly, but before he could fasten the first buckle, he felt something cold and hard slide up the back of his shirt.

"What? Who?" he managed as he tried to turn. But he was suddenly hoisted high into the air.

Roughly eighteen to twenty hands high, he thought as he realized what had happened. One of the other unicorns had slipped its horn up inside his shirt and was lifting him up.

"No!" he shouted. "Bad unicorn! Put me down!" Though he was relieved the horn had not actually gone into his skin instead.

That unicorn showed no sign of hearing him. But someone else did. On the other side of the thorn bushes that Aspen could now see over, he watched as someone broke for the trees. He was wearing a long cloak in patterns of dark green and black that had obscured his shape when he had been still. A large floppy hat in the same patterns obscured his features. He was slipping quickly and with a certain amount of practiced ease toward the pines. But he was not as quiet as he thought.

Aspen watched the man only for a moment, because as the runner reached the pines—which pointed toward the limitless sky—his cloak helped him fade into them as if he were a part of the foliage.

There was also a large crash from off to the left that distracted Aspen. It sounded like a boulder rolling through the woods, taking down trees as it came. *Except the boulder must be bouncing,* Aspen thought, *because it seems to be thump-thumping as well.*

"What? Who?" Aspen said again, still dangling from the unicorn horn, this time looking for the cause of the big noise.

The rest of the unicorns all had their heads up to look as well, fully alert and making short, breathy, houghing sounds to one another as if conferring.

But when the cause of the noise came crashing out of the woods, they reared as one, trumpeting their terror, using both their mouths and horns like a band of great braying bugles. The one who'd speared Aspen's shirt flung him aside like a terrier who had finished worrying a rat.

As Aspen spun through the air, he was unable to tell which way was up. But even so, he recognized what had burst out of the woods and had time for one shout of warning to the camp before he hit the ground.

"Trolllllll!"

SNAIL TO THE RESCUE AGAIN

*B*efore the scream had finished leaving Aspen's throat, before his head had hit the ground, sounding like a limb falling from a dead tree, Snail was on her feet and running. She cared little if the professor was running, too, or the dwarfs scrambling, or the unicorns fleeing—all of which seemed likely.

As she ran, she stumbled over a tree root, crunched one of the hobbles underfoot, stubbed her toe on something hard she didn't see, but still made it to Aspen's body before the troll could. She stood before him and held out her hands, palms up and forward.

Not in supplication. No one in their right mind would plead with a troll. Her heart, banging away, reminded her of that.

"Stop right now!" she shouted as if scolding a child with a finger too near a flame. "Stop it!" Her voice didn't even quiver, which surprised her as much as the troll.

The troll stopped. Eyes asquint, jaw jutting, her tusks

nearly vibrating with shock, she glared at Snail. Then she put a meaty hand to the baby strapped to her chest. His bottom half was wrapped in an oddly familiar striped diaper.

"Huldra?" Snail said, suddenly recognizing the troll.

"Midwife?" the troll said, a bit whiny, like a toddler deprived of a sweet.

"Remember the troll's pledge!" Snail snapped, surprised—at herself, at the troll. "No eating a midwife. Especially not your midwife."

Stopping any troll in mid-hunt is always a chancy thing, even a troll one knows well. Even a troll a midwife had recently helped to birth a baby. Even then.

And of course there was Aspen to consider. A prince. A knight. Most ballads about knights and trolls ended badly. In fact, now that Snail thought about it, *all* ballads about knights and trolls ended badly. Her heart was thudding out danger warnings so hard in her chest she was afraid it would burst through the fragile shield of skin. When she'd seen Aspen on the ground and the troll heading in his direction, she hadn't given fear or danger a moment's thought. She'd suddenly had the strength of several grown men. Midwives called it a *knighthood flush*, as females in labor—whatever size and kind they were—suddenly found themselves filled with courage and strength.

Though now, in this moment, the *only* thought she had was, *Prince . . . troll . . . this isn't going to end well. Think, Snail, think.*

"Yes," she said carefully, "I'm your midwife, and he . . ." She stepped to one side and pointed dramatically at Aspen, who was just starting to sit up, though he looked as if he'd had the breath knocked out of him, and his face was ashen. "He's my apprentice. A midwife's apprentice. You remember him, don't you? He helped at your baby's birth. So you can't eat him, either." She was relieved that he wasn't already dead, but not yet convinced he wouldn't be troll breakfast soon.

"Well, I will eat *him*!" said the troll, pointing behind Snail.

Slowly, so as not to alarm Huldra, Snail turned her head. The troll was pointing to Professor Odds, who stood there looking a bit amused and not at all alarmed.

"I wouldn't do that if I were you," Snail said, turning back to the troll. "He's a wizard and could bring up the sun before you took two steps toward him. And then— well, you know what would happen then." She shrugged dramatically. *Everyone* knew what happened to trolls if the full-risen sun shone on them.

"I turn to stone." Having offered that sentence without any sign of fear, Huldra suddenly flung herself down on her knees, careful not to fall forward onto the baby, but she was so mammoth and so heavy, her weight opened a small fissure beneath her. Now she looked unbearably sad. "I wish I *was* stone," she said. "Hungry. So hungry."

Fully awake, Aspen was still white-faced and now looking confused. Snail wondered briefly if he'd landed on his head.

She glanced at Odds, who seemed to be waiting to see what would unfold next. Somewhere from the forest came the sounds of unicorns munching on the undergrowth, obviously convinced the danger had passed.

Simpletons! Snail thought. *Troll danger is never over . . . till it's daylight.* She had no idea where the dwarfs were now. Or Maggie Light.

Never neglect the mother, came Mistress Softhands' voice in her ear. It was good advice, even if the mother was an unhappy, hungry troll.

Or maybe especially then! Snail thought.

She put her hand on baby Og, strapped to Huldra's chest. With the troll on her knees, Snail could reach that far up, though she had to stand on her tiptoes to do so. "What's wrong, mother? Why have you left the cave?"

At that Huldra began to weep the way only trolls can: great globular tears inching from her eyes and grey snot like the trail of a real snail, only giant-sized, tracking from her nose till it was stopped—*barricaded,* Snail thought—by her chin bristles. Then the troll took a deep breath and howled.

With that, baby Og began to howl, too.

Not thinking, Snail reached out to the knot in the sling under Og's bottom, untied it, and took him in her arms. He was scarcely ten days old and already as big as the bogie toddlers that kept the Unseelie castle free of mice. And cats.

With an effort, she began to rock him till he stopped cry-

ing at last and started giggling instead. Then he fell immediately to sleep with a hiccupping snore. The striped diaper
was wet all the way through.

"Snail," came a whimper from behind her.

Without turning, she hissed, "Shhhh. Don't say another
word, Prin . . . er . . . 'prentice, or I'll personally feed you
limb by limb to this poor starving troll."

There was a deep, darkening silence behind her. She
couldn't tell if Aspen was angry, frightened, or dead. But at
least he didn't speak again.

"Now . . ." She said the single word in the calmest way she
could, though she felt neither calm nor sure it would work.
Her next words were hardly calm at all, tumbling out of her
like a river in full spate. "The apprentice is fine, the baby
is fine, tell me what's troubling you, Huldra. And then we
will find you a cave or a cabin nearby where you can sleep
during the day." She stopped and took a deep breath, ready
to say more.

"Not sleep. Hungry. No food. Two days." Huldra's big
hands clutched her belly.

"You *must* eat for the baby's sake," Snail told her. How
often she'd heard Mistress Softhands tell a mother that.
Well, actually three times, she thought. The first had been an
ostler's wife who had the after-birthing wobbly-cobbles. The
second, a drow's wife upset that she'd only had four babies
and not six, which meant her husband would beat her and

possibly eat her or, failing that, throw her out of the nest. And third, a pretty young Border Lord's wife who wanted to get up out of her birthing bed to go riding with her man.

"There is no food for me. No . . ."

"Why doesn't . . ." Snail tried for a moment to remember Huldra's mate's name, but gave up. "Why doesn't your mate hunt for you?"

Even as she said it, she recalled the pitifully small rabbit he'd come home with when she and Aspen had just helped Huldra give birth. Surely the mate wasn't much of a hunter.

"Ukko is . . ." And then Huldra's blubbing began anew, only this time, tears and snot fell like a storm threatening to drown Snail, baby, and all.

As Huldra rambled in between wiping her nose with an increasingly messy sleeve, Snail listened and thought about next steps. And she kept bouncing the baby to make sure he stayed asleep.

"Those jerker berserkers, those skirted scourges, those sword-waving hordes, those roguish brogue-ish monsters . . ." Huldra said.

Suddenly Snail saw it: The baby is diapered in a swatch ripped from a kilt. Huldra is talking about the Border Lords. Of course.

Just as Snail had that realization, Huldra's story stumbled out of her gigantic mouth. She'd been in the forest doing an evening of berrying, the baby safe in Ukko's arms back in their cave, when a troop ("Scouting party," Aspen amended from behind Snail, but she didn't take time to admonish him) must have stumbled onto the cave.

"Probably drawn there by the smell of a haunch of venison cooking on an open fire," Aspen whispered.

"Hush!" This time she turned to warn him. But he was probably right. The cave in the Hunting Grounds where the trolls lived gave off magical odors to suit any prey's desire. She'd smelled cabbage soup, and Aspen had smelled roasted nuts and honey. "Let her continue. We don't have all night." Or at least the troll didn't.

"So the Border Lords . . . er, the jerker berserkers found your cave, and then what happened?" Snail asked.

Another mammoth wailing cry, and then Huldra said, "Ukko fought bravely, but one of the little swords . . ."

Nothing little about those swords, thought Snail, knowing even a Border Lord had to use two hands to wield one, but didn't say it aloud for fear of stopping the story's flow.

But there was no fear of that, for Huldra was now herself the river in spate and nothing was going to stop her till the tale was done. "My handsome hulking husband, the lofty love of my life, was kicked and pricked by the kilted cult and died defending our son. Our Og."

Aspen said, "What did you do then?" before Snail could stop him.

"I ate them, of course."

Snail felt sick at the thought but worked hard at not showing it.

"I had not time to boil them. Nor the heart for hot food. Not with dear Ukko so dead."

The conversation was not going the way Snail had hoped. "And then?"

"And then I buried Ukko. . . ." Here Huldra gave another, shorter wail accompanied by more snuffles. "It was a waste of meat, of course, but troll takes too long to butcher properly. It has to hang . . ."

"Huldra, enough. And then . . . ?"

"And then I set out with little Og before more of that awful tribe could find us. Only . . ."

"Only what?" Snail prompted.

"Only I'm not the hunter Ukko was and I am so, so hungry." She looked once more at the professor and at the two male dwarfs, who now stood on either side of him, and the female, who stood in front of him, her fists raised.

"Don't worry, Huldra," Snail said, "we'll get you something to eat."

"We will?" asked everyone but Huldra.

Huldra just grinned. It was not an improvement.

"The little folk will hunt for you," Snail said, waving at the three dwarfs.

Aspen shook his head and got to his feet, still a bit shaky. "They dare not. All deer in the forest belong to the king. Taking a king's deer is called poaching and any poacher caught is immediately hanged without trial or jury or sentence. Without recourse to a legal advisor or a last meal or time to say farewell to his family."

"Or hers," Dagmarra said. "So we will be careful not to get caught."

"There," Snail told him. "Satisfied?"

"You do not understand," Aspen said, giving up all pretense of not sounding like a toff. "The king's deer are all under an enchantment. If shot by anyone not of royal blood or without magical dispensation to hunt deer—like the king's huntsmen—they give off a signal like the ringing of a bell. It sounds back in the Royal Forester's hall and lights up a magical map to show where the deer—or its corpse—is heading. There is no escape from those foresters. They are silent, swift, and final. They are bred for it."

"So that's why no one poaches here!" mused Dagmarra. "I always wondered . . ."

"Then what's *your* plan?" Snail asked Aspen. She'd given Huldra her assurances that she would be fed.

But as swiftly as she spoke, she wished she could have taken it back because she knew what Aspen was going to say. It was that old noble and honor stuff that he kept spouting.

"I will go," Aspen said.

"You can't, you're a minstrel," said Annan at the same time Huldra said, "You're a midwife's apprentice."

"He's a prince," spat Professor Odds. "Anyone with half a brain can see that."

Huldra looked up expectantly. "So, can I eat him?"

"No, dear," Snail said quickly, before Professor Odds could answer. She was afraid he'd say yes. "Who would hunt for you then?"

Professor Odds went on as if no one had spoken. "It's a fact I've known for some time. In fact, for the sum of time he's been the Hostage Prince, the one who's started this war." He stared pointedly at Aspen, daring him to contradict him.

Aspen stood up straight and proud, though he was obviously still shaken from his fall. "And will end it, too," he said, "or be killed as I try."

Strangely, Snail was proud of Aspen for saying that, even as she shook her head. "We're *all* likely to be killed as you try." She was glaring at him again. "But first go get the troll her deer."

"Two," Huldra said. "Two deer. I have to eat for two, you know."

"Not anymore, dear," Snail said in her best imitation of Mistress Softhands in her scolding mood. "That's only for when you have not yet given birth."

"I will need a bow," Aspen said.

"And arrows, too, I suspect," said Dagmarra.

Just then Maggie Light came gliding across the clearing with a large bow and a quiver of arrows.

Dagmarra spit expertly to one side. "Always anticipating."

"That is my calling," Maggie Light told her. "It is what I am made for."

Snail wanted to ask what else she was *made* for, but held her tongue. There was something about Maggie Light that was . . . off. Not right. Odd. Even odder than Odds. But this was hardly the time to find that out.

Smiling, Aspen reached for the weapons, but Maggie Light held them back.

"Perhaps you should wait till you are steadier?"

"Noooooooo!" howled the troll. "So. Hungry."

Aspen looked at Snail and she shook her head. "Best not."

With a sigh, Aspen pushed himself to his feet, slung the bow and quiver over his shoulders, and trudged to the forest edge where the unicorns still munched the undergrowth. He stumbled slightly as he walked.

Snail realized he was still wobbly from the fall. Watching him disappear into the woods, she wasn't sure whether to be angry he'd revealed himself, worried he'd get hurt while hunting, or afraid he'd take too long and Huldra would eat the rest of them before he returned.

She ended up feeling all three things at once. Which didn't feel good at all.

ASPEN HUNTS AND
GETS SMALL THANKS

*A*spen marched into the woods, following a stream, his head aching, his steps a bit unsteady. He had never actually hunted deer before, but he could certainly use a bow, and he knew a tiny bit about deer, thanks to Jaunty.

Deer like to drink in the evening before their night grazing.

Jaunty had told him that at some dinner long ago. The high table had been served venison, and the smell of the food was, for once, divine. As he had only been at the Unseelie Court for less than a year at that point, and had not had his Seelie seventh-year growth spurt yet, he had been barely able to peer over the table. Even perched on several pillows so he could eat, the meats were piled too high for him to see his dining companions.

Just as well. Even after a year, he still was not used to the oozing and warts and general grotesqueness of the Unseelie nobles, and he found it hard on his appetite to look at them while eating. But he kept his eyes on Jaunty, who was not unsightly, only old.

"What do you think of deer?" Jaunty asked, pointing to the venison on the platter.

He remembered answering Jaunty happily, "Deer like to be put in my belly!" Jaunty had laughed his distinctive high titter and given his young student a friendly pat on the head. That was one of those few good memories from his time as a hostage, a time that otherwise had made him uncomfortable and sad.

I wonder if Jaunty is even still alive? he thought. *My running off may have sealed his fate. The king would have had him tortured into a confession and then killed. I wish I had figured that out before. I could have persuaded him to come with me.*

But of course he knew that was nonsense. If he had told Jaunty, the old tutor would have been honor-bound to report it.

And then he had an even more horrific thought. *If the Border Lords are in the Hunting Grounds, then war has truly begun.*

His thoughts began to spiral downward in a maelstrom of misery.

Who has died so far because of me? Who else will die while I pretend at minstrelsy and poach my father's deer?

Pausing and listening, he answered his own question: *All of us will die if I don't get that troll fed.*

He heard nothing, just birds singing a last chorus before full night. So he moved on, heading farther upstream.

A few hundred yards, where the stream turned south, he stopped again. This time he thought he heard movement up ahead and he pulled the bow off his shoulder and then an arrow from the quiver. He could not believe how easy it had been to track the deer.

But was it deer?

Or could it be a bear or a lion or a charging boar? Were the arrows in his quiver strong enough and sufficient for killing a predator? The questions tumbled through his head with no answers following them, like deer fleeing an incompetent poacher.

Only then did he remember the hidden watcher. The man in the green-and-black cloak. Maybe *he* was the one making all the noise. *Could he just have been innocently relieving himself and then been frightened off by the ruckus of the unicorns and the crash of the troll?*

Aspen didn't think so. *That cloak.* That cloak had been designed for keeping the man hidden. And for spying.

But who was he spying on? Me? Odds's troupe? The troll?

He bit his lower lip. It seemed unlikely that anyone would want to spy on a humbug magician, a trio of dwarfs, an animated rug, a mysterious, beautiful lady, a midwife's apprentice—and especially not on a troll.

Besides, how many wars have any of them started lately?

He thought about turning around and going back to camp. He needed to warn the others about the watcher.

But returning with no food for Huldra seemed an even

more dangerous proposition. If he was to face the mysterious stalker, at least he was armed and Snail was in the company of friends.

Strangely, though that should have been a comforting thought, he found that he wished Snail was here with him, facing whatever was making all that noise around the bend in the stream.

Probably Snail would stand shoulder to shoulder with me, a knife in her hand and a scowl on her face, he thought and chuckled silently.

Notching the arrow, he slow-walked quietly to the bend in the stream and sidled up to a maple whose branches stretched halfway across the water. He knelt down and peered carefully through the leaves.

There was just enough light left for him to see a half dozen deer, all females, dipping their heads and drinking while a big stag kept watch farther up the bank.

If I could get two shots off quickly, he thought, *and if I hit both targets . . .* Suddenly he started to tremble with anticipation, and the arrow began to wobble.

Slow, steady, he warned himself. *Take a deep breath.*

He was suddenly struck by another thought: killing the deer was one thing, hauling them to camp by himself another.

With that in mind he picked out the two smallest females as his targets and aimed at where he thought the heart would be.

Firing from his kneeling position, he took the first doe in the chest. It fell as if struck by a spell.

"Oh!" he gasped. He had done it. Done it!

Then he stood and stepped out of the maple's branches as the herd began to scatter. Keeping his eye on his second target, he reached back for an arrow. Then sighted along the arrow's length.

The second deer he chose bounded back and forth recklessly. For a moment he considered sending magic after it, but knew that—even though the magic anti-poaching spell that was on the deer would not be triggered because he was a Seelie prince—with two armies after him, any spell he cast could be noticed and traced.

He breathed out, opened his fingers, let the arrow go.

It missed the deer by two hands' breadth.

He pulled another arrow from the quiver, and another, and shot them after the fleeing deer, barely stopping to aim now, knowing that with the distance and the deer's jumping and jolting, he just had to put arrows in its vicinity and hope the doe leapt the right way.

Or the wrong way, if you are the deer.

The doe jumped into the path of the fourth arrow, and it hit her in the throat. She stumbled a few more steps, then fell down.

Aspen tried to remember the Seelie prayer of thanks to Great Nature, but it had been too long or he was still too addled from his fall, so silently he heaved one carcass onto his shoulders and grabbed the other by a hind leg, and began a long, dragging stomp back to camp. Dusk lasted till near midnight in Seelie lands, but still he doubted he'd make it back before full dark.

❖ ❖ ❖

No one was there to welcome him into the clearing. The unicorns, hobbled by better hands than his, were still munching contentedly on the thorn bushes and did not even look up.

But movement from one of the wagons caught his eye.

It was Dagmarra standing watch.

Or rather sitting *watch*, he thought, for she was perched on the wagon's seat.

She jumped down and, without a word, picked up the larger of the two does and slung it over her shoulders.

And it dwarfs her, Aspen thought, laughing silently at his own wit, before realizing he was thinking like an Unseelie prince.

"Thank you for the help," he said quickly.

She grunted in answer, before adding, "We've just about run out of starters for her meal."

Together, they hauled the deer to the campfire, where the Professor had set up a mobile kitchen. Supplies had been dragged from their storage under the wagon, and a clever, collapsible table stood ready with knives sticking magically to a dark stone inlay along its side. There was a spit over the fire and several large pots that each looked capable of cooking a small dragon.

Huldra was sitting on the ground hunched over, but even when she was sitting, her head grazed the lower branches of the trees. Her baby was asleep in a cradle made out of a barrel that had once housed apples. Or at least that was what the sign on the side of the barrel said: ESKER APPLES; ONE BITE WILL CHANGE YOUR LIFE.

Around the troll was all that was left of several pounds of carrots, a sack of potatoes, and the shells of what must have been two dozen eggs. He wondered if she had eaten all the Esker apples as well.

"At last," said Huldra, reaching for the larger of the two does. "I was about to start on her." She pointed to Maggie Light, who simply smiled back at the troll as if harboring a great secret.

"Touch one hair . . ." Aspen began, but beside him Dagmarra laughed. "Don't worry about her," she said. "She's *klebarn*."

"Klebarn?" He had never heard the word, trollish or otherwise, and wondered if it had to do with her ability to sing spells. But he had no time to puzzle it through before Huldra began stuffing the deer—head first—into her cavernous maw.

She ate it whole.

And raw.

Aspen was disgusted. Professor Odds, on the other hand, seemed fascinated.

"I've never had the opportunity to observe a troll's eating habits before." Professor Odds pointed at Huldra's throat. "See how she swallows the hunks of meat, much like a wolf. Barely any mastication at all!"

"Yes. That's . . . um . . . interesting," Aspen said, peeved that no one, not even Huldra, had thought to thank him for bringing back not one but two deer—though Huldra could be forgiven since she was, after all, a troll.

He glanced around for Snail but she was nowhere to be seen. *Maybe*, he thought, *she is elsewhere sleeping. Or . . .* He could not think what other things she might be doing. *And really*, he told himself, *I don't actually know much about her besides the fact that she's a midwife's apprentice, very argumentative, and . . .* He gave himself a mental shake. *Be fair*, he told himself. *She is loyal, honest, and brave, and likes me. Well*, sometimes *she likes me. Other times she just glares.*

Still, he wanted to tell Snail about his successful hunt for the deer. And about the cloaked man.

But first he needed some sleep.

Looking at Odds, Aspen said, "I think I'll go to my room."

"Not hungry?" Odds laughed a peculiar sniggering sound. "Then your room is a splendid idea. And ideal . . ." He waved his hand in Maggie Light's direction without taking his eyes off the troll. "Maggie, get Prince Karl's supplies for him. Then supply me with my sketchbook. Take the long way around to the bowser's room. No need to disturb the others."

"My *supplies*?" Aspen asked.

"Oh, didn't anyone tell you?" The professor finally looked at Aspen after Huldra swallowed her last section of the first deer and had started on the second, smaller doe. "You're to clean the bowser. The rug in your room. It's waiting. In fact, it's lying in wait, though it weighs hardly anything at all. And having no tongue, never lies. Though, of course, it lies around all the time. There's a riddle there, prince, if you can but read it. If you are good at unriddling riddles."

"Professor Odds, with all due respect, I have been injured, I am exhausted, and since you have made clear that you know of my station, the respectable thing would be to—"

"Station!" the professor interrupted, snarling. "You have no station *here*, boy!" He leaned in, and though he was looking up, Aspen got the impression that Odds was looking down his nose at him. "The troops after you endanger the troupe I look after. And endanger that perfectly respectable girl who follows after you." He gestured toward the wagon.

Which, Aspen thought, *could mean Snail is anywhere.*

Odds completed his rant: "If she didn't care for you I'd leave you in a ditch without a care, having ditched you."

Aspen was agog. Not even in the Unseelie Court had anyone spoken to him that way. Even when King Obs said he was going to kill him, he had said it politely. When the twins Sun and Moon had teased him, they did it within the proper form. The Border Lords called him names, but never anything a prince could not bear. And though the assassin boggarts in the Unseelie dungeon had spoken roughly, it was to one another *about* him. Even with a knife at his gut, they would have given his station all due respect. So why was this highly educated professor not treating him with respect?

Professor Odds glared at Aspen for another moment before Maggie Light returned.

"Ah, my sketchbook," Odds said in a normal tone, and turned back to sketch Huldra with the second deer partially down her throat, its white tail waggling between her tusks at each gulp.

Aspen stared daggers at the professor's back but could not think of a single thing to say on his own behalf.

At last, he admitted grudgingly to himself, *He's right—I am endangering all of those around me. But especially Snail.*

Turning to Maggie Light, he said as politely as he could manage, "And my tools?"

She handed him a bucket and brush, then led him around the wagons to enter it from the front.

SNAIL LEARNS SOMETHING

*S*nail was hard at work in Maggie Light's room, learning to take apart and put together a puzzle.

Odds himself had set Snail that task, soon after Aspen had disappeared into the woods. He had guided Snail into his room, leaving Maggie Light to feed the troll what she could. Once there, he picked up something shiny off his desk. The shiny thing was a dense cube, about the size of a cooking apple.

Then he led the way into Maggie Light's room, tossing the cube back and forth between his hands. Once there he set the cube down on Maggie's dressing table, where it was reflected in the silvered mirror. Then he'd settled Snail into the dressing table chair, and turned on a magic lantern to illuminate all the pieces.

The cube and its reflection seemed to shimmer.

Twice as mysterious that way, Snail thought.

"Hand on the puzzle," Odds commanded.

"Puzzle?"

He bent over, then placed his pointer finger atop the silver box. "Tell me what you see, what you feel."

She bent forward until her nose practically touched the box. It seemed to be made of several metals, some silver and some a bit darker. She told him so.

"Good. What else?"

She touched the box as he had, with a single finger. "Cold."

"Yes?"

"And . . ." She rubbed all the fingers of her right hand except her thumb across the surface of the box. "Smooth," she said, before hesitating. "Though not, I think, entirely smooth. Little small runnels, or hair's-breadth creases. I think . . ."

"It's good to think. Continue until you can take it apart."

"It comes apart?" *Doing so might be amusing,* she thought, *some other time.* Out loud she asked, "But shouldn't we be back helping with the feeding of . . . ?"

"Maggie has everything under con*trol*." Odds laughed at his little joke, which seemed to Snail no joke at all.

"But professor, a puzzle . . . at *this* time, with a hungry troll eating up your stores and a war about to break out, you want me to take a puzzle apart?"

"We'll feed the troll from our stores," Odds said, "enough to stave off the worst of her hunger till the prince comes back with the dweer. Maggie Light and I have the least to fear from her."

"Huldra won't eat *me*," Snail reminded him. "Trolls are pledged not to eat midwives."

"If this is indeed war," retorted Odds, "all pledges are considered void. Finished. Done with. And if she gets hungry enough, even a midwife would make a tasty morsel." His pointer finger poked at the puzzle.

"But you and Maggie . . ."

"Our magic, alone or combined, will not be overcome by a troll who has nothing but brute strength on her side," Odds said. "Now this is what I want you to do . . ." His pointer finger poked at the puzzle and pushed it closer to her.

Snail couldn't take her eyes off the cube, but she didn't reach out for it again.

"Don't make me regret taking you in, girl. You are as much of a puzzle as that bit of iron and silver. There is no time like the present. I am offering you a present of time."

"It's made of *iron*? But . . . it will burn me." She wondered why it hadn't already burned her. Or him. She assumed it had to be his magic. That would make him a very potent magician if true because cold iron burned every fey.

Or he was lying to her. About the iron. About . . . everything.

"It will not burn you," he said.

"It will." Snail turned her stubborn face up at him. And her glare.

"Trust, my girl, is the first step."

Snail shook her head, but he didn't seem to notice.

"And of course the puzzle comes apart," he continued. "Anything that is made can be unmade. Just do not wrench any of the pieces or bend them out of shape, because later I will have you put it all back together."

"But why . . . ?" Snail persisted.

"Some whys do not make you wise," Odds said, "though you will be wiser later."

Snail's head was spinning with questions, but she only managed one more. "Is the box worth a great deal, then?" She didn't take her eyes off it as she spoke.

"It's not more than its price but less, which is to say it's priceless," he said, which was an answer that was no answer at all.

He stood and went over to the door. "Oh, and I shall want to know how you planned what you will do and how long it takes. Call me when it is fully apart. And each part fully noted. There is a piece of paper for your notes. You do know about notes, I hope. And not the kind you sing. And sing badly, I warrant."

She wondered if he was simply giving her something to do to keep her safe and away from Huldra, or just busy and out from under his feet. Or if the box thing was some kind of test. Though what kind she couldn't even begin to guess. And why she should be tested was a fact even further away from anything she could guess at.

She was still trying to figure it out, when the door closed behind Odds with a short *snick*. Startled, she felt as if waking from a spell. Snail stared down at the box until she stopped thinking about the reasons Odds had given it to her, and became fully engaged in the process of taking it apart.

Quickly she realized three things.

First, she was already beginning to see the fine lines she'd only felt beneath her fingers. They reminded her of fault lines on a mountain road. Shaken or tapped the wrong way, crevices could open big enough to swallow a cart and carter whole.

Two years earlier, the apprentices at the Unseelie Court had had a day off to go into the mountains, and such a fault had opened up in the road. Cart and horse with all their food for the day had fallen in. They'd scrambled away from the road, some screaming, some weeping, some dragging away friends. Luckily the carter had escaped. Or luckily until he was put in the dungeon by an angry Bonetooth, the half-ogre chef of the Unseelie castle kitchen who'd complained to the king's account keeper about the loss of cart and food. Nobody had cared about the horse, an old spavined creature on its last legs anyway, which would soon have been a meal for the drows and woodwose. But its screams as it fell in had invaded Snail's dreams for many nights after.

She guessed her best hope to open the box was to concentrate on those fault lines.

Second, she knew she'd be needing finger dexterity. That didn't worry her. How many knots had she practiced tying under Mistress Softhands's watchful gaze? Seven years' worth before she'd been allowed to tie off the cord that ran between the ostler's wife and her newborn child. And how many scissors had she taken apart and put together again till Mistress Softhands was satisfied she could do it in a dark cave or a candlelit byre, with or without a tool to help. And how many fine cuts had she learned with the vast array of midwife knives—some as thinly bladed as a fingernail and as curved, others as straight as a string stretched between fingers.

That left the third thing: What was her plan, where and how to begin? And what kind of notes would satisfy the professor?

She hefted the box in her left hand and threw it into her right, then back and forth as she'd seen Odds do, nervously and quickly in case of a burn. Next she gave the box the slightest shake. Closing her eyes, she let her right fingers glide across the box's surface again, still a bit warily until she realized that Odds was right. It didn't burn her. Which meant either the thing wasn't iron or Odds's magic still held even though he wasn't present.

Or three, she thought, *I really* can't *be hurt by cold iron*. She dismissed that idea at once. Everything she'd ever been told about the fey trembled on that answer being false.

This time she knew what she was looking for. She did that whole routine twice more, and each time she could feel the fault lines getting slightly larger.

When she opened her eyes at last, she found she could

see the largest line when she squinted at it. Putting the box back carefully on the table with the lines at the top of the cube, she began massaging the face of the box in different directions.

She pretended she was massaging the belly of a woman in labor as Mistress Softhands had taught her, with a broad, consistent, slow touch, though—unlike the bellies she'd massaged before—this surface was hard, cold, and hadn't the pulse of life. As she did so, the almost invisible lines became entirely visible, turning quickly into a crack, then a crevice large enough to stick her pinky in.

After that, the thing came apart easily, but she slowed down enough to be sure she arranged the pieces on the table in groups so she would know how and where they could be put back together. Then she made careful notes, of the kind she'd done for each birth she'd attended with Mistress Softhands, though not that last, disastrous birth where the queen of the Unseelie Court had killed one unfortunate apprentice and consigned the rest of their group to the castle dungeons.

And not, of course, she thought, *when Huldra gave birth to Og, there being no paper, no pen, and no time for any such.*

Snail had no idea how much time had passed. But when she went back into the professor's room it was to learn that Huldra had finished the last gulp of the second deer, the dwarfs had been sent off to check on the unicorns, the professor and Maggie were taking notes in a book with the title

Of the Eating Habits of Wild Trolls scrawled across the top of the page.

Oh—and baby Og was beginning to stir in his apple barrel cradle.

"I've finished taking it apart," Snail said, wondering idly where Prince Aspen was since clearly he must have been the one who'd brought Huldra the deer. Funny, how she hadn't heard a thing. He couldn't have been *that* quiet about it and she was only just next door.

It's just like what happens in a birthing room, she thought. *Intense concentration on one thing leading to a kind of deaf-blindness to everything else.*

"We're all but finished here as well," said Odds. "Let me come and see how well you've done."

ASPEN DOES SOME CLEANING

*A*spen stared bleakly between the bucket and rag that Maggie Light had handed him and the furry *thing* he was supposed to wash. He had been distressed enough being forced into a servant's role—again! But he was prepared to clean the rug with as much energy as he could muster.

The rug had other ideas, sprouted teeth, and growled at him.

"The bowser does not like to be washed."

Aspen jumped in surprise at the voice coming from what he had thought was a long, grey cloak hanging on a strange rack. But then he saw pale eyes in the recesses of the hood and pale, knobby fingers just peeking out of the sleeves.

"And I most assuredly do not want to wash it," he replied. He wanted to add, *A task well below my station . . . or below my former station. The professor has made it perfectly clear that I hold no station here.*

Something about the creature seemed familiar, but he could see so very little of it, he could not figure out what it was. *Seelie? Unseelie?* "But that is the task I have been set."

He stopped for a moment, remembering something his old nanny had said: Work ennobles. He hadn't understood it then, of course. He must have been five or six at the time when she said it. But now, suddenly, he *did* understand: Sometimes the noble thing to do is the lowest thing. Like helping Snail in the cave as she midwifed the troll baby into the world. Which led directly to Huldra the troll not eating anyone in Odds's troupe. *This, at least, is a step up from a troll baby's birth!* he thought. *Though on second thought, maybe not!*

"The bowser respects firmness," said the cloaked creature.

Aspen nodded and took a cautious step forward, bucket before him as a shield. "I can be firm," he said without much conviction.

"But not too firm! The bowser appreciates a gentle hand."

"Firm but gentle. I understand."

He took another step forward and the bowser rippled down the middle like a sheet being puffed out by a maidservant. Then the row of fearsome teeth reappeared in the front, and Aspen stopped, shaken.

Firm.

"Stop it, bowser!" he snapped, trying to speak in the deep, strong tones he remembered his father using with the castle hounds. He sounded squeakier than his father ever had, but the bowser stopped rippling.

However, its teeth were still bared.

Now gentle.

Aspen forced himself down to one knee, his face now alarmingly close to the creature's mouth. He could see it had multiple rows of teeth like the large predators of the northern ocean. Only smaller, of course. Not that he had ever had the opportunity to see the large predators or the northern ocean, but he had read about them in his studies with Jaunty. And there had been one rather horrific illumination in the book. He had always thought it exaggerated. He was no longer certain. The back rows of the bowser's teeth looked ready to swarm forward if any of the front ones failed in any way.

Gentle but firm, he reminded himself.

"See here, bowser. I do not want to wash you, and you, apparently, do not wish to be washed." He knew that might sound indecisive to the bowser. And possibly to the other creature in its shapeless cloak as well.

"Nevertheless, bowser, that is exactly what is going to happen. Best if we do it quickly and quietly with as little fuss as possible." Dipping the rag into the bucket, he swished it around. All the while he hated the greasy feel of the thing and wanted to remove his hand from it. But he did not.

Remembering his father with the hounds, holding out leather leashes for them to sniff, he held the rag up now so the bowser could examine it.

Though the thing has no eyes that I can see. No ears either,

but it obviously knows I am here. The teeth are proof of that.
He may have been imagining it, but the jaws did not seem
to be gaping so wide after his little speech to the creature;
the teeth *were* a bit more hidden.

Aspen squeezed the rag a little so he would not slosh cold
water onto the creature. *We definitely do not want to shock it,
now.* Then he leaned forward and pushed the rag into the
middle of the bowser's . . .

Back? Surface? Floor? Aspen did not know what to call it;
he was just glad the animate rug made no move to bite him.

"There, that is . . . that's a good . . . erm . . . bowser," he
cooed, and began scrubbing. The surface of the creature
was rug-like, but a great deal warmer, and it moved occasionally under his hand as a hound might. Aspen went back
for more water, then scrubbed another spot.

The brown of the—*fur? fabric?*—turned near black with
the moisture; but after scrubbing for a few minutes, Aspen
looked over at his earlier work and saw that the part of the
bowser he had washed was drying to a shining gold.

"You really *were* filthy!"

The bowser rippled as if in response and finally closed its
toothy jaws.

"I believe you may have made a friend."

Aspen had almost forgotten the cloaked creature, and
turned his head toward it.

"Perhaps." He shot it a quick grin. "We shall see when I
wash near the mouth."

He moved to where he'd last seen the teeth and scrubbed there now. There was no sign of teeth—front or back—and he felt no sign of anything hard or pointy beneath his rag.

Interesting.

And suddenly he was done. Only a few spots of dark remained as the bowser's heat dried the final wet patches, and it looked for all the world like a rug of spun gold, a gold that seemed to light up the room.

"Why—it is . . . beautiful," Aspen said, unable to disguise the awe in his voice. "Fit for a king's chamber."

The cloaked creature stepped forward and reached down, stroking the back of the bowser with long, skeletal fingers. "Is it?"

Close now, Aspen smelled the sweet stench of overripe fruit and remembered where he had seen this kind of creature before.

"Sticksman!" he shouted. The bowser rippled backward and gave a halfhearted show of teeth, before quickly settling again.

The cloaked creature turned its gaze on Aspen, and he recalled clearly the same pale blue eyes of the skeletal creature that had poled Snail and himself from the Unseelie lands across a river filled with carnivorous mer. They had not had enough payment for passage, and Aspen had promised the Sticksman a favor in exchange for the ride. He remembered that favor now. It was his geas, his fate, and he spoke it softly to himself: *You will travel far and you will meet crea-tures old, odd, and powerful. You will ask each of them these three questions.*

He asked the first questions aloud. "What is the Sticks-man?"

"The Sticksman?" the creature asked Aspen. "What is that?"

Aspen bit his lip. It was an old childish habit he thought he had overcome. Ever since Old Jack Daw had told him it was a *hsssko*—in the drow language, a "tell" by which players of the game of Chancer read another player's face to know what chits he held in his hand—he had tried to lose the habit. He let his face go bland, but inside he felt empty. He had been so certain of the creature.

"Sticksman," he repeated. "Just something I thought you were." He no longer had high hopes for his three questions, but he would ask them anyway, for after all, the promise had been given.

Even if he was late in remembering.

"What is the Sticksman?"

"I asked *you*, man, because I know not," the creature answered.

"I suppose, then, you do not know how he came to be?"

It was the second question.

He/she/it cocked a skeletal head. "If I know not what it is, I deem it unlikely I would know how it came to be."

"Then I suppose," Aspen said, "asking how the Sticksman could come *not* to be is right out?" That was the third question.

The creature shook its skeletal head, which made an alarming creak, and looked away.

"I have a question of my own," Aspen said suddenly.

"The other questions were not yours?"

"They were given to me."

The creature nodded. "Then they were yours."

"Yes . . . um . . . no! Or, yes, I do not know. I do not think it is important."

The creature nodded some more as if Aspen had made sense, though he felt he had begun to babble.

"Anyway, my *new* question is this: What are *you*?"

The creature straightened and pointed to the far end of the room. Aspen looked and saw another identical cloaked creature he had not noticed before. Or if he had noticed, he probably thought it just another cloak hanging on a hook.

"My sib and I . . . " the creature said, pausing mid-sentence while its sib raised a skeletal hand in what started as a wave but ended in an ambiguous upturned palm. "My sib and I . . ." the creature began again, "we are so old, our names have passed from the minds of all creatures—even our own."

"Truly?" Aspen thought that seemed both likely and unlikely, he was not sure which.

The creature and its sib nodded.

"Then what are you called?"

"Why should we be called?"

"I mean, if someone wants you to . . . to . . . come quickly."

The sib joined them, walking silently, as if its feet did not touch the floor. It said, "We do not come quickly." But indeed it had.

Aspen tried again. "Well, should I want to introduce you . . ."

"Sometimes," said the first creature, "the professor calls me *You*."

"And sometimes," the sib said, "he calls me You, Too."

"And sometimes," they said together, "he calls us They or Them or Those."

"And when he is with Maggie Light, he calls us the Trio," said the sib.

"Though we are not three but two."

"And the last two of our kind," added the sib.

"Actually," Aspen said, smiling up at the tall creature, suddenly sure, "I believe there *are* three of you. But Maggie Light is not one."

A sudden hush filled the room, as if eternity had entered, but before either creature could speak further, the hush was broken by a snore. The bowser, so long ignored, had fallen asleep at Aspen's feet.

The snoring reminded Aspen of how tired he was.

Seeming to recognize that, one of the twins said, "You should rest," and almost at the same time, the other said,

"You have walked a long way, hunted through the night."

Together they added: "We can talk of this on the morrow."

That sounded good enough for Aspen. At least some-one—some*ones,* he reminded himself—recognized all that he had done through the long night. He *did* deserve to rest. Not caring whose bed he collapsed onto, he pulled off his boots. Within minutes he was asleep.

But somewhere, in the middle of a dream in which every-one was screaming, he woke up.

SNAIL MEETS A MAN WHO
WASN'T THERE

$\mathcal{S}$nail had all but finished putting the box back together.
There were three pieces left and none of them seemed to
fit where there was room for them. She was wondering idly
if she would have to take everything apart again and start
anew. Half of her hated the idea, and the other half thought
it would be fun. In fact, the most fun she'd had since . . .

Since . . .

Had she ever *really* had any fun? In the Unseelie castle
there had been the occasional dance and tipsy cake and par-
ties with the other apprentices, but for some reason they
weren't as much fun as they should have been. And there
had also been beatings and Mistress Softhands's small
magicks that had turned her into various animals as punishment, once even into an actual snail. And there had been
Mistress Treetop's withy wand, which had left many a red
mark on Snail's arms and hands for being sloppy at her
work. And the Border Lords, who liked to grab young girls
and toss them back and forth for sport. And the dungeons.

And the troll dungeon master, who—she had discovered only recently—had very sharp knives and . . .

Fun in the Unseelie world was not for the likes of girls like Snail. Hard work and dodging blows were always more in abundance than pleasure.

She sat with the three metal pieces in her left hand, thinking, *But* this *has been fun.* She couldn't think why.

And then suddenly, it wasn't fun anymore.

Fun is for toffs, she thought, *not for us. What is Odds thinking, anyway? If he knows who Aspen is, then he knows we're hunted by both kingdoms. He should help us fight or hide or run away.*

Then she had a frightening thought. *Maybe he's waiting to turn us in.*

She thought about that for a few seconds, then shook her head. *He wouldn't. Or rather, he would have already if he was going to.*

She started to slam the three pieces down on Maggie Light's bedside table, then stopped. She wasn't quite sure enough to risk breaking them.

Whatever his plans, she thought, *he shouldn't have me playing games and solving puzzles.*

Sighing, she put the pieces down carefully and went outside for some air.

It really had *been fun.*

❖   ❖   ❖

IT WAS A full moon outside of the wagon, and one of the dwarf brothers was sitting watch. Snail couldn't tell which one. He waved pleasantly and patted the seat beside him, but Snail shook her head. She didn't feel like talking to anyone. Didn't feel like even looking at anyone, so she plastered a good-natured grin on her face, returned his wave, and walked to the back of the wagon.

Where I can mope in peace.

There was a soft cooing of doves overhead, and from farther away she could hear the contented sounds of the unicorns as they munched on the occasional thorn bush and the whisper of their hooves as they moved slowly through the grass.

She'd barely had time to sit down on the back runner, hadn't time to think anymore about the Odds problem, when a thin arm snaked around her waist and something cold and sharp was pressed against her neck.

Snail took a shallow breath and was about to yelp, but the blade pressed farther into her neck and a voice whispered, "Quiet, now, pretty girl, we do not want to rouse your friends, now do we?"

That's exactly what I want to do, she thought, but gave a very small nod instead.

"Now, stand," the voice said, the arm around her waist tugging her upward. The voice of her captor was soft, smooth, yet hard, like a rock that had lain long under a rushing river.

"And if you are a good girl—as I am sure you will be without any more need of persuasion—I will tell you what happens next."

"All right," she said. She wished she were still wearing her midwife's apron with its pockets filled with knives that were easy to get to. Her entertainer's outfit didn't have any pockets at all, and her knife was riding in the small of her back in a sheath sewn right into her skirts.

It's closer to him than me at the moment. She didn't know if that was going to change. *Or how many more moments I am likely to have.*

"You are going to call to Prince Astaeri and have him meet you back here."

She almost didn't know who he was talking about till she remembered Aspen's actual full name and title: Prince Ailenbran Astaeri, Bright Celestial, Ruire of . . . something, and Second or Third successor to . . .

Well, almost remembered, she thought. *But who calls him that?*

She couldn't look down at the arm around her waist or the hand holding the knife without getting cut, but she bet if she could, she'd see hands that were covered in gaudy rings and expensive bracelets. The way he used words—that stiff, stilted language—and the way he treated her like so much dirt told her everything she needed to know.

Well, almost everything.

"You're a toff!" she almost shouted it but switched it to a

whisper as the blade at her throat stung her, drawing blood.

"Quiet!" he hissed. "It matters not what I am, it only matters that you follow my instructions."

It matters not, she thought. *Definitely a toff.*

"You are going to call to the prince. When he arrives, I will trade you for him and we will be gone."

Trade me? she thought, her head abuzz with questions. *Not likely. I'd raise a cry. He'll kill me. That's what toffs do to inconvenient underlings. But if he's a toff, why isn't there a whole troop of soldiers here? Why only the one man?*

Then she had it. "You're not taking him to Astaeri Palace, are you?"

Snail's captor chuckled, though there was no humor in it. "Sadly for him, it is not in the cards. His fate will be worse at King Obs's keep, but my reward will be greater."

Snail knew he was right. The Seelie Court would hang Aspen and be done with it. King Obs would have him tortured in the dungeon for many days before turning him over to the Border Lords, who would do even worse.

"My reward for his capture in this kingdom would be a small promotion and perhaps a mention at court."

"But King Obs," she said, "will give you your weight in gold."

"More, actually. A lieutenant's pension or a prince's ransom? I will live the life I should have had instead of this. Thus it is an easy choice. Good for me. Sad for the prince."

His hold on her was less tight now, as if he expected her

to obey just to win free of him. As if she prized her own freedom over Aspen's. Which, in a way, of course, she did. But in a way—which was her only advantage—she didn't.

"Now, call to him."

Snail knew the man's plan would work. If she called, Aspen would come out quietly, and when he saw the situation he would naturally do the *noble* thing. He would give his word and force Snail to promise she wouldn't follow and he wouldn't even try to escape after that.

Stupid, stupid, stupid, Snail thought. *No matter that he'll be tortured and killed. He'll do the noble thing. The stupid thing.*

Then suddenly, she smiled, thinking, *I can be stupid and noble, too.*

"No," she said, quietly but quite firm. "I won't."

"What?"

The knife was definitely drawing blood now. Snail could feel a few drops running down her neck and over her chest. She hoped it wouldn't turn into a river soon, but she wasn't hopeful.

"I said, no." She was very afraid and very angry, but she was strangely happy.

Maybe this is why Aspen does the noble thing. To feel like this. She realized she was now actually grinning.

"I won't call to him," she went on. "You can kill me, but then you'll have nothing to bargain with." It suddenly dawned on her why he was grabbing her and not Aspen himself. "And you don't want to face him, do you? He's always armed, and besides, he has his princely magic and you're just a lowly foot soldier with a great-aunt who married a cousin to a chancellor or some such thing."

Her captor groaned as if he and not Snail was the one with a knife at his throat.

"Shut up!" he nearly shouted, just barely remembering to keep his voice down. He spun her around and punched her in the stomach. Not too hard. After all, he needed her up and able to call out.

First she was out of breath. And then she was furious. She hated being poked in the stomach. And punched was even worse.

"Don't *do* that!" she said, and glared, though even with the moon, he probably couldn't see it all that well in the dark. But at the same time, she got her first good look at him.

He was dressed in a long cloak. *Green and black,* she thought, *though it was hard to tell. And wearing a ridiculously large floppy hat. He had the half-slanted eyes of the toff clans, and their sharp cheekbones, the thin gash of mouth.*

As sharp, she thought, *as the knife still in his right hand, still too close to me.* Her anger had faded and now she was thinking hard. And fast.

The cloaked man's body seemed too bulky for his thin, elven face, and Snail suspected he wore armor underneath the robes.

"Listen, now—" he said, the voice still full of authority.

But by facing her, by loosing his hold on her waist, without the knife pressed to her neck, he'd lost the advantage, Snail realized. So she smiled at him, and nodded as if going along with his plan, all the while noticing that, as she expected, though he was dressed for subterfuge and fighting above, he was wearing a pair of expensive, beautiful, and very comfortable boots of the finest thin doeskin.

Very thin doeskin.

Suddenly and unexpectedly, she stomped on his foot with all the anger and fear he'd caused. She felt the foot scrunch beneath hers, ground down hard, thought she heard a bone—*make that bones!*—crunch.

The man leapt onto his other foot screaming and Snail jumped back, finally able to reach the knife at her back.

"Karl!" she yelled, screaming along with the man. "Help! Help! Help!"

Huh, she thought, *I guess I will call to him after all.*

ASPEN GETS ALL NOBLE

*A*spen rushed outside and around the back of the wagon because that's where the sounds of shouting were coming from. Rocks and twigs pressed into his bare feet and he immediately regretted not putting on his boots before leaving the wagon.

Regretted it, that is, until he saw Snail. She was struggling with an elf much taller than her who was dressed in a cloak patterned in black and green.

Our silent watcher! The stalker!

The man had a short skinning knife in his right hand, and Snail was holding on to his right arm with two hands, trying desperately to keep him from plunging the blade into her chest.

"Snail!" Aspen roared, forgetting immediately what her new name was supposed to be. He felt a rage come upon him, and he could suddenly feel faery magic swirling around him. He had but to reach into its core and pull out lightning or fire and destroy this creature that dared hurt his only friend.

No! he thought, fighting for control. *Use the magic and far worse than this one elf will soon be on our doorstep.*

He remembered a quote from a famous Unseelie general that Jaunty had shared with him long ago: *It's easier to keep control while moving forward.*

The general had been talking about his armies, known more for their mad, violent charges than their discipline and skillful soldiering. *Just like Border Lords.*

Aspen was neither Unseelie nor in the army, but he thought that the same principle might very well apply here. Besides, he wasn't going to be able to formulate a better plan in the few seconds he had before Snail was overpowered. And killed.

So he charged, but silently because he was barefooted. At the last minute, he dropped his shoulder to ram into the cloaked man's side. It was then he noticed Snail's knife sticking into the elf's hip and thought, *Good girl,* just before they all fell to the ground.

Snail scrabbled away and then everything devolved into a scrambling mess of fists and elbows.

Aspen had no experience in this kind of fighting. *But the stalker is already injured so perhaps I have an advantage.*

At the same time, he thought, *I have very little experience in any kind of fighting at all, come to that.* As a Seelie prince, he would have been expected to lead men into battle eventually, but as the hostage prince, he had only been expected to stay put and keep the peace.

And look how I failed at that, he thought, anger and misery binding together.

Still, guessing that this type of fight would be won by the combatant who kept most active, he flailed around with fists and elbows and knees in the fervent hope that the watcher's knife had been knocked aside and was now lost in the darkness.

Something caught him a glancing blow to his chin and he lashed out in the direction it had come from. His fist connected with something hard and he heard a satisfying grunt as his knuckles exploded with pain. He was not expecting it to hurt and for a moment he was stunned by how much it did.

Then he and the cloaked man were in tight and grappling, and Aspen tried to find the man's neck so he could squeeze. But his opponent had the same idea and found Aspen first, though Aspen ducked quick enough that only his chin was under pressure.

Finally certain where his opponent was—if still not entirely sure which way was up—Aspen launched elbows at a location sure to hold a stomach or some kind of vital organ, but oddly the arm suddenly disappeared from around his neck and his elbows found only air.

High ground! he thought, remembering that as a key component in warfare. It was one of the random things he remembered from the few lessons his father had given him in warfare before shipping him off to the Unseelie Court. He wasn't certain what the high ground did for you, or how it applied here, but he decided that in this case it meant that he should stand up.

He pushed himself to his feet, swinging around to where the silent watcher should be, and realized that the elf had also taken the opportunity to get to his feet.

Unfortunately, he'd also drawn a long rapier from a sheath at his hip.

Before Aspen could do anything but gasp, the watcher stepped forward in a beautiful lunge and pierced Aspen's left arm straight through. There was weakness but no pain as the arm went slack, and Aspen found himself back on the ground, looking up at the elf, who was poised to pierce his heart as well.

One part of Aspen wanted to close his eyes to his own death, but the other part—the noble part—forced him to keep his eyes open.

The Seelie motto on the royal banners was *Look death in the eye*, though he suddenly remembered his mother telling him before he was taken off to be the hostage prince, *Look life in the eye, too.*

Fine words, he thought, but there was little hope for life now when a sword was about to end it.

Be brave, be brave he told himself over and over. *It will be but a pinprick, and if I am lucky, will hurt but a second.*

In the middle of his prayer a truly odd thing happened. Sword drawn and pointing at Aspen's chest, the cloaked man suddenly had a very surprised look on his face and flew straight up and away, his cloak billowing around him like a giant bat's wings.

He can fly? Aspen thought. *That hardly seems fair.* He tried to remember anything about flying Seelie elves and failed.

Then the pain in his arm hit him, and the only sensible thing to do seemed to be to black out completely.

SNAIL AND THE HUNGRY TROLL

It all happened so fast, Snail thought. One minute she was going to die and the next minute it was Aspen who was dead, or so she thought until she saw his hand fluttering.

Somewhere overhead she heard the cloaked man sputtering and pleading, starting to scream. Somewhere overhead she heard the troll droning, "Hungry! Hungry! Juicy man."

But Snail ignored all the screams and scuttled over to Aspen, whose eyes had just been fluttering open.

"Am I dead?" he asked.

She looked at the wound in his arm, just above the elbow. It was hardly bleeding. "Not even a little."

"Good," he said. "It was not a very noble fight."

"The intent was noble."

He smiled and it was the sweetest smile he'd given her since they'd met.

She glared back and with her knife cut off his bloody sleeve.

"Don't do that again," she told him. "We've got to get through this together. Agreed?"

What she could see of the arm in the moonlight showed a wound that was deep—had gone all the way through, actually—but had somehow managed to miss all muscle and bone. If cleaned and bandaged, the wound shouldn't give the prince too much trouble.

Aspen began to sit up. "Agreed." He said it as if he meant it, as if there were no chasm between them, no deep gaps of birth, of class, of education, of futures.

"Then . . ." she began.

But there was a terrific thud behind them. The ground shook and a baby with an enormous pair of lungs began to cry nearby. It was the kind of crying that could knock birds from the trees and make grown men weep. It could curdle milk and make cows' udders go dry. It could . . .

"Huldra?" Aspen said.

"Og?" Snail said.

They both turned at once.

Huldra was stretched out on the ground, blood flowing freely from a deep cut in her leg, probably as far as the cloaked man's sword could reach. Snail knew that such a cut, if it had hit a major vein, could make the troll bleed out in a minute.

Or maybe two. Snail tried to remember what she'd learned about blood loss from the midwives.

Then she had it:

One minute royals,
Two minutes lords,
Whether from breakage
Or tusks or broadswords.

Three minutes Red Cap
Who pays the blood tolls,
Four minutes boggarts
And ogres and trolls.

There were four more verses, of course. But it was clear that she had but a little time to save Huldra. Less than four minutes if the rhyme was true. Aspen's wound was minor in comparison, so she would have to let him be on his own for now.

Midwives, like all carers, knew the rule:

Who bleeds the worst,
We care for first.

That worked for new babies and their mothers as well as their husbands or mates who may have hurt themselves in the aftermath of the birth by celebrating too much or fainting at the sight of either birth blood or the after-clots.

"Amazing," Mistress Softhands often said, "how men who have wounded or killed in battle pass out when their womenfolk bleed."

"Here . . ." It was Dagmarra at Snail's right side. She handed Snail a bunch of the white wooly fluff from a clump of lamb's shear growing nearby. "You can use this to staunch the wound, and save a bit for putting in your ears. In fact, you should probably do that first."

Instead, Snail used the entire two hands worth of the fluff on Huldra's wound and then wrapped it tight to her with strips torn from her last petticoat. It would do until Snail could stitch together the vein.

She suddenly recalled how she'd used the top petticoat when delivering baby Og. *This is getting to be a habit.* But she'd never liked those petticoats anyway, silly useless things. *Well,* she thought, *not so useless when used as bandages.*

Baby Og! He was no longer bound to Huldra. But she could hear him screaming. "Where is he?"

Dagmarra said, "The minstrel?"

"The baby. *Where's the baby?*"

Dagmarra pointed dramatically toward the wood where Aspen had gone hunting for the deer. "Don't worry. Prince Noble is off saving the baby!"

"But he's . . ." Snail spun around to look at where Aspen had just been lying on the ground behind her. He was gone. "Just injured," she ended lamely.

Dagmarra had squatted down and was plucking more of the white cotton fluff. "This time put these in your *ears.*"

"We need to help Asp . . . Kar . . . er, Prince Noble."

"Maggie Light will take care of that," Dagmarra said, stuffing her own ears. "Best you do this, too."

Suddenly, Snail remembered when the soldiers had first come looking for them and she'd watched through the strange window in the cart. Obviously, Maggie Light's voice held some kind of magic spell. So she stuffed the cotton in her ears and walked around the troll to see if she could find Aspen.

He was standing near the first wagon, both of his arms wrapped around Baby Og, whom he'd apparently just pulled away from the cloaked man.

She wasn't worried until she saw that the cloaked man's right arm was around Aspen's neck. Aspen, who didn't dare let the baby go to fight his enemy, didn't seem to be faring well.

In fact, his face was darkening. Probably turning blue. In the half-light of the Seelie night, it was hard to tell.

Dimly she could hear the cheers of the dwarf brothers behind her, through the stoppers in her ears. Running over to the two struggling men, she grabbed the baby from Aspen's hands and held it close to her chest, where it wriggled and kicked and was not at all happy. She hoped that having a free hand now would give Aspen a bit more leverage in his fight with the bigger man, even with his arm wound.

"Og! Og!" she said loudly to get the infant's attention. "I'm not here to hurt you but to rescue you."

Not seeming to be at all convinced, Og kept on kicking and flailing his arms. Snail spun around, found Odds and Maggie Light, who were standing by the trees.

"Sing!" she shouted. "For Mab's sake, Maggie, *sing*!"

Maggie Light nodded, held her arms up, opened her mouth, and began to sing.

Snail could hear only a bit of it, garbled through the wool, but with her one free hand, she pushed the wool even deeper into her ears to shut the rest of it out.

Already Aspen and the cloaked man had gotten strange looks on their faces, and both had begun to sink to the ground, though they were still clutching each other. The minute they landed, their hands dropped to their sides.

Og had stopped wriggling in Snail's arms, and began to smile the way all babies do when fast asleep, a bit of milk drool falling off of his bottom lip. The drool would have filled a flagon.

At that moment, Dagmarra came strolling over with a long rope in her hands and bound the cloaked man's hands behind him. Then, with a vicious twist, she tied the longest end around his ankles as well. Grinning, she turned to Snail and mouthed, "Hobbled!" before pulling him over on his back.

At which point Maggie Light stopped singing.

Despite her wound, Huldra came haltingly toward them, plucking handsful of white fluff from her ears.

Not so deep a wound, then? Snail mused, remembering

what Mistress Softhands had warned about birthing trolls: A troll is never more dangerous than when she's bloodied. It's why the magic rule about not eating midwives was first laid upon them.

Huldra bent over to get a good look at the captured man. She prodded his belly with a massive forefinger. "Good for ribs," she said. "I eat."

"You can't . . ." Snail began, her own stomach roiling at the thought.

"I eat," Huldra said again. "Builds strength. Will make me strong. I must be strong for Og."

"We . . . we . . ." Snail tried to think of what to say, but Odds spoke as he came out of the wagon.

"We shan't be barbarous," he said, pushing his thin, grey hair back against his scalp. "Though we could use someone to barber us. No one is eating anyone."

He approached the prisoner as if he expected everyone to move out of his way. And they did, even the hungry Huldra, who eyed him with a mixture of anger and fear as she shuffled off a little distance.

Odds stood over the bound elf and for a moment stared down before nodding to Maggie Light.

"Wake him."

She gave a short whistle and the prisoner woke. Aspen, too. The prisoner tried to shoot to his feet, but was caught up in the knots Dagmarra had tied and fell, catching his face a scraping blow on a tree root. Aspen just lay there looking exhausted and in pain.

"You alone?" Odds asked the prisoner.

"Of course not, you fool!" the prisoner shouted as he struggled to a seated position. "I have troops waiting for my signal. If they do not receive it soon they will swoop down on your encamp—"

Odds nodded. "He's alone. Such boasting comes from fear."

Snail watched the cloaked man slump, all the bravado leaching out of him like wine from a burst wineskin. She wondered how Odds could have known for sure, wondered if it was just a good guess. Knew it wasn't the moment to ask.

Odds went on. "You came for the prince?"

The prisoner nodded agreement.

"What do you know of me and my company?"

"Nothing."

"Truly?"

The prisoner shook his head. "You are not what you seem. But what you are, I do not know."

"Yes," Odds said, though what he was agreeing to Snail couldn't tell.

Odder and odder, she thought. She had a few questions of her own she wanted to put to the cloaked man. And to the professor as well.

But Odds nodded to Maggie Light, who immediately knelt beside the prisoner and sang a short, sharp note into his ear. He fell back limply, his face relaxing for the first time since Snail had stomped on his foot.

It took her a moment to realize that he would not be moving again. Ever.

"You killed him!" she said, too stunned to do more than whisper.

Odds looked at her blankly. "What else would you have had me do?"

"Question him more."

"I know all I need to know about him," the professor said. "More than I want to know. He was a small thing. With a small mind. And we should mind him no more. Besides, he would have been a constant thorn in our sides as we travel on and would have had to be watched day and night. You pluck thorns out, not shove them deeper into the skin."

"But . . ." Snail began, "you can't just kill a tied-up person like that."

"They do it to us without giving it a thought. Without thinking what we're due." He glared at Aspen. "Isn't that right, *Prince*?"

Snail stared at Aspen, who didn't say anything aloud. But he gave a single short nod toward the professor, clearly agreeing with him.

She glared at him and then at Odds and finally at Maggie Light, who looked back at her with a sad expression.

"Dear one," Maggie Light said, "there really was no other way."

"Maybe so," Snail said, "but you two didn't even try."

"I wasn't made to try," she said. "I was made to do."

Nothing makes sense, Snail decided. She stomped over to Huldra and handed her the baby, then, suddenly sick to her stomach, she ran to the bushes, afraid she was going to throw up.

Once she was in the bushes, the sick feeling went away, but all Snail could think of was how empty her arms felt now. And how empty her heart felt, too.

Without a word more, she made her way back in the wagons, and went into Maggie Light's room. There she picked up the silver box puzzle and flung it against the wall.

Let the professor pick up the pieces, she thought. *I'm through with them all.*

ASPEN FACES THE ODDS

*A*spen followed Snail into the wagon, hoping she would dress his wound. But when he saw her smashing Maggie Light's stuff, he backed out before she saw him and headed to his room. The twins were gone—perhaps helping to bury the cloaked man.

His arm aching, Aspen sat on the floor, and the bowser sidled up and put a corner in his lap. He scratched its golden fur idly as he tried to puzzle through what had just happened with Snail.

I do not understand why she is so angry about the watcher's death. He tried to kill her. And me! She should be glad he is gone.

But when he had nodded his head agreeing with Odds's decision, her reaction had certainly not been one of gladness. Nor was it her usual summer-storm fury that came on swiftly but passed just as fast. The glare she had shot him was more regret than anger, as if she finally saw him for who he truly was and was deeply disappointed.

But clearly there was no other logical solution! We did not torture the watcher, nor let the troll eat him—all niceties that the people he was going to sell me to would not have bothered with. He died quickly and without fear or pain, and we can all go about our business with clear consciences.

Still he felt uneasy, as if his conscience did not actually feel all that clear.

"Why is she mad at me?" he said aloud. "I did nothing wrong."

"Come," Maggie Light said, "let me bandage your wound."

Startled, Aspen looked up. He thought he had been alone. Well, alone except for the bowser. "Um . . . thank you, my lady."

She knelt next to him and began wiping the puncture in the front of his arm with a clean, damp rag before working around to the wound in back where the rapier had come out. It should have hurt as she scrubbed, but she hummed a light tune that made him feel disconnected from his body. Also, he realized, being this close to a woman so heartrendingly beautiful was distracting as well. Especially one who seemed to value him, as Snail did not.

He sniffed her hair surreptitiously, but smelled nothing. Where most women would have doused themselves in an attar of aromatic flowers, bathed in the smoke of burning herbs, or glamoured themselves up a pleasant scent, Maggie Light seemed to have no scent at all. Not the earthy musk of a peasant girl who worked the fields all day, nor the soapy cleanness of a midwife's apprentice, nor the artificial but usually more pleasing scents of the aristocracy.

His arm twinged as Maggie Light pulled the newly applied bandages tight around it. The pain made Aspen snap out of his reverie and back to himself.

"So," he said, not wanting her to leave, "where did you learn to sing that way? And who taught you the songs that . . . um . . . do those things?"

Maggie Light stood and looked down at him quizzically. "I didn't learn anything. I am klebarn."

"What is a klebarn?"

"It is what I am."

This is starting to feel like talking to the Sticksman, he thought, the one who had told him: *You will travel far and you will meet creatures old, odd, and powerful. You will ask each of them these three questions.* But when he had asked the questions of the twins, they had known nothing.

Maggie Light didn't seem all that old, but she was certainly odd and powerful. And he had never had the time to ask her the questions before. Perhaps this was the right time.

"Tell me, Maggie Light," he began, "do you know what the Sticksman is?"

Eyes closed, she thought for a moment. Then her eyes opened and she said, "He is the Unseelie boatman who ferries passengers from the Water Gate at Unseelie Castle to the Unmastered Lands."

Finally, someone who knows what I am talking about,

Aspen thought. *Though I do not think that the Sticksman is Unseelie.*

"And how did he come to be?"

"I was not given that knowledge."

"Do you know how he would come not to be?"

Maggie Light shook her head. "That knowledge would flow from the knowledge I do not have. How is the arm? Better?"

He flexed his arm. Wiggled his fingers. "It will serve."

"Can you use a bow?"

He pulled his hand back to his ear as if drawing a bow and immediately pain and weakness shot through his arm. "Doubtful."

Maggie Light cocked her head momentarily as if listening to a distant voice. "Then Professor Odds will want to speak with you."

"How can you—"

"When I am given knowledge, I do not question it. I only do."

Aspen was not sure whether that was a good philosophy or even entirely what she meant, but he took her hand when she reached out to him and pulled him to his feet. He let her lead him outside and around to Odds's office.

❖ ❖ ❖

"I KNOW YOU noticed we have no musicians," Odds said without preamble as Aspen entered. Maggie Light waited outside. "That's how you thought to burrow your way into our company, stealing what you couldn't borrow. A wolf in a mole's skin." Pausing, perhaps awaiting an answer, he sat at his desk, a thin sheaf of papers in his hands.

"We didn't mean to burrow or borrow," Aspen said, "only to seek shelter."

"No matter, no matter. But to get to the *meat* of the matter, it matters that we'll soon have no meat."

For the first time when talking to Odds, Aspen thought he knew what the man was talking about. "I cannot hunt, so Huldra will soon eat us out of supplies."

"To wit: Being out of supplies, Huldra—who is too weak to hunt—will soon eat us. So we need to kill the troll or get supplies."

Aspen knew Snail would never forgive any of them if they killed Huldra. Especially so soon after killing the watcher.

Odds nodded as if Aspen had spoken the thought aloud. "We need a way to get supplies before we become them. A way your kind is most unfamiliar with." He grinned. "We'll have to work for it."

"That is unfair, professor. Did I not just hunt two deer and wash the bowser and . . ."

He stopped. *And what else? Before that, what else have I ever done that could be considered work? My food was cooked and served to me. My apartment and clothing kept clean for me. My bath drawn for me. A horse saddled for me. In truth, until I escaped the Unseelie castle, I had done nothing for myself, nor was I expected to.* But perhaps as Hostage Prince, his was a special case.

Be honest! he warned himself. No nobleman or toff—even *he* was beginning to think of them by that name—was expected to do anything like work.

What about soldiering? War is upon us, and the lords are expected to lead their soldiers into battle! Mouth open to say this to Odds, he stopped again. *And then the lords bravely watch from the rear as the conscripted—the poor, the unlanded, the farmers and laborers armed mostly with spades and scythes—slaughter each other.* Yes, if things went very badly, the toffs might be expected to wade in and take a distasteful swing or two of their bejeweled weapons at the shuffling hordes. But even in warfare they were not expected to *work.*

Finally, having demolished his own argument, he nodded his agreement.

Odds looked at him strangely, as if he had expected a different reaction. Then he went on. "Both our musicians and a number of our players rode on ahead after our final show. So we are one actor short for our production of *Eal, Ollm, and Fydir.*"

Aspen was familiar with the famous play about Princess Eal, the dragon Fydir who kidnaps her, and the brave Prince Ollm who rescues her.

"I thought *final* production means—well—final."

"We'd brought along enough foodstuffs to get to our

destination without performing again," said Odds. "But we weren't trolling for a troll. I never wanted to lose control like that again, thank you very much. I—"

Aspen took a chance and interrupted. "I thought that *Eal, Ollm, and Fydir* is a three-person play. Surely you have enough people in the wagons—what with Maggie Light and the dwarfs and the twins and . . ."

"When I said 'a number of our players rode on ahead,' the number I was thinking of was 'most.'"

"And the others?" Aspen was not going to let go of it.

Professor Odds sighed. "The others are needed to keep the crowds in order, do the music, take tickets, guard the wagons."

"So you want me to play Prince Ollm?"

"An obvious choice."

"I am not trained in the acting arts, but I think—"

"But not a possible choice," Odds interrupted. "That role is taken."

"By whom?"

"Dagmarra."

"Oh."

"You could try to convince her to play a different part."

Aspen thought about that. "Has anyone ever tried convincing Dagmarra of anything?"

"Yes."

"How did that go?"

"I'm certain they're fully recovered by now."

Aspen shuddered. "The dread dragon, Fydir?" he said hopefully, then remembering two lines from the play spoken by the dragon, added,

> I bluster, I fester, I blow,
> and down your castle will go!

Usually children of the Border Lords cheered at those lines. Sometimes, as a boy, Aspen had cheered along with them.

Odds shook his head.

"Maggie Light—"

"Doesn't act."

"Snail could—"

"She has a different task."

"The twins?" Aspen said desperately. "The dwarf brothers?"

"Don't be frivolous." Odds handed Aspen the sheaf of papers he'd been holding. "The princess's lines are here. But they should be here—" He pointed to Aspen's head. "Before midday on the morrow. Which, judging by the moon, has already become today. It always does, you know."

"Memorize the lines by midday?"

Odds nodded. "And Maggie Light will fit you for your costume. So you will be more than fit to play."

Aspen shuddered at the thought, which made Odds smile.

"Come, Your Serenity," he said. "You'll finally be dressed

appropriately to your station. Meet Maggie in her room."
He pointed to the door, then turned away, a clear signal
that the meeting was over.

Aspen left through the indicated door, and walked into
Maggie's chamber, where she had already laid out a selection
of frilly, brightly colored fabrics for him to choose from,
knowing he would have agreed to play the role.

"Breeches and a shirt from the orange?" he asked hopefully.

Maggie Light smiled prettily. "The orange it is."

They both knew it would not be breeches she planned to
sew.

SNAIL TALKS TOUGH

*M*aggie Light found Snail a while later. She was sitting curled up on Maggie's big bed, her head in her hands.

"Do you wish to speak with me?" Maggie Light asked.

Snail was silent.

"Or will you hear what I have to say?"

If anything, Snail was even more silent. No permission given for or against.

I'm no longer here, Snail told herself. *I've already left. Or at least I will leave once it's light.* She knew that courage was one thing, stupidity another. And the definition of stupidity would be wandering around in a forest at night all by herself with two armies, Border Lords, and a hungry troll close by.

"Though you may not think it now," Maggie Light continued as if permission had been given, "the professor is a great man, greater than you can ever know."

Snail houghed through her nose, sounding, she knew, like one of the unicorns.

"He is willing to make the hard but necessary decisions," Maggie Light said.

"Like telling you to sing the cloaked man to his death?" Snail bit her lip and thought, *I didn't mean to talk to her, or to anyone. Just get up at first light and leave.*

"And to let the troll eat the spy as well," Maggie Light added.

Snail sat up. "He didn't!" Her voice was sharp, even shrill. "She didn't!"

"The professor did. The troll did." Maggie's face looked neither happy nor sad at what she was saying. She only looked . . . beautiful.

"That's . . . that's. . . !" Snail couldn't think of what to call it. But began to shake with anger.

"That is the only logical decision that could have been made. Think about it, girl: We have a dead body, a prince who cannot hunt for us in the enchanted forest because he has been wounded, and not enough stores to get us to where we are going without a hungry new mother troll devouring us one at a time because she, regrettably, is hungry and has no husband or anyone else who can feed her." She stopped, and drew a breath, though not one Snail could hear. "It is not the troll's fault or our fault or . . ."

"It's just *wrong*!" Snail said. Her indignation turning to anger, she glared at the singer.

"It just *is*," Maggie Light told her. "And only one person could make that decision quickly, decisively. The spy's death will mean another day or two of life for Huldra and Og."

"And then?"

"And then we will be at the fairgrounds and will perform and—hopefully—with a good crowd, we will make enough coins to restock from the fair merchants for the rest of our trip."

"But Huldra will still be with us." She thought, *I don't really mean* us, *because we aren't us anymore. The closer we get to daylight* . . . "And she will still be hungry."

"Yes. But by then she may be able to go back to the Shifting Lands, where she lived before. Since they are not under the Seelie king's magic, she can possibly hunt for herself and her child. Or return over the bridge to the Unseelie lands, where she can possibly find another mate." Maggie Light smiled again. "So you see . . . many things can happen now, whereas before only one thing was possible and this the professor understood as no one else could."

"All I see," Snail said, standing, "is that no good comes out of bad."

She walked to the door that led to the next room, away from Professor Odds's room. Opening the door, she turned and said over her shoulder. "And following one wickedness with another is bad addition."

"Bad addition," the bird squawked from the next room. "Two wrongs! Bad addition!"

As she went through, she heard Maggie Light call after her, "There are many things more in mathematics than addition." Snail didn't know if she was answering her or the parrot. "That is why the professor is the one who makes the hard decisions."

She might have said more, but by then Snail was no longer listening.

❖ ❖ ❖

SNAIL FOUND ASPEN dozing in the twins' room, lying on top of the golden rug. Without disturbing him, she glanced at his arm, but there was no blood soaking through the bandage. Someone had obviously made a good job of it, so she left him to sleep. It was the best medicine at this point.

In the next room, where the dwarfs' small beds were crowded together, the bird called out to her, "Pay the troll."

"We've already paid the misbegotten troll several times over," she told it. "We're out of coins. Out of patience. And out of time."

As if happy with that answer, the bird put its head under its wing and promptly went to sleep.

❖ ❖ ❖

ONCE OUTSIDE, SNAIL found the dwarf brothers sitting toe to toe on the raised platform, pipes in their mouths. Over their heads circled little curls of smoke that resembled dragons with tails in their mouths.

On the far side of the meadow, the unicorns still grazed

noisily. Near them, Huldra and Dagmarra were walking along, taking turns playing with baby Og, throwing him up in the air between them. His laughter rang out like bells.

The whole scene—unicorns, the happy mother troll, her new friend, the gurgling baby—threw Snail into another fit of anger. No one seemed to care that something awful, something truly terrible, had just happened there.

Nobody but me, she thought.

Grumpily, she went back into the wagons. There was nothing to do but go to sleep. She was sure to have bad dreams.

This time, as she passed by Aspen, the bowser growled and showed about a hundred sharp teeth.

She growled back at it so ferociously, it shut its mouth.

The prince stirred, opened his eyes, mumbled her name.

"Oh, go back to sleep," she said sharply.

Her tone really woke him up.

"Snail," he told her, "we cannot stay here longer. It is too . . . too . . ."

"Too awful." She knelt quickly and actually checked Aspen's wound this time. It was already scabbing over and there seemed to be no redness or infection at all.

"Too dangerous," he whispered. "What if Odds has Maggie sing *us* into a final sleep next?"

"She wouldn't do that."

"She told me she does not question what Odds tells her to do, she just does it."

Snail couldn't disagree. She already knew that was the truth. "Go back to sleep. The sleep of the brave." Then she added, "I'll sleep as well. We're both too exhausted to think properly right now. We'll make plans in the morning."

Our plans, she thought. Suddenly, it had a nice ring.

ASPEN AND THE BEST-LAID PLANS

*A*spen woke in pain. His arm hurt from the sword wound. His head hurt from his fall. His knuckles hurt from the one punch he'd thrown that had connected.

I think the rest of me hurts just so as not to be left out.

He got to his feet while trying not to move any appendage too swiftly nor rock his head about in any way. It was made difficult by the fact that the wagon was in motion. But he must have been successful because he didn't immediately fall back over.

On the bed next to him lay a formal gown in orange with pink trim. In his size.

"Oh," he said. "Ow."

Staring at it made his head feel worse, so he stumbled from the room. He had no destination in mind at first; he just wanted to get away from the awful dress. But when he found himself at the front of the wagon, he realized that he was hoping to find Snail. He knew she liked to take the air with the dwarfs up front whenever the wagon was moving. And though it was still dark, they were already moving forward.

Suddenly, Aspen remembered why he wanted to see Snail and have a quiet word.

She was perched on the front with the two dwarf brothers, looking refreshed from having gotten some sleep. Or from the fresh night breeze blowing off the mountains. Or maybe it was from the full moon, now almost gone behind the near hill, burnishing her face, making her look ethereal.

Though actually, he thought, *it is probably the prospect of leaving the wagon and escaping into the wilds again that has brought color back to her cheeks. At any rate, she looks far better than she did last night, when she was so drawn and pale.*

She spotted him emerging from the wagon and shouted, "Halloo!" before he could give her a silent signal to come and talk. "You having trouble sleeping, too?"

The dwarfs looked up at her hail, and when they saw who it was, grinned at him.

"Did you see the costume Maggie Light made you?"

"You'll be *dressed* for success," Thridi said.

"No skirting the issue," Annar added.

Aspen waited for more, and was surprised when that was all they had to say. "Come now," he said, "I expect better from the two of you."

Annar gave a theatrical sigh. "It's early yet."

"The professor had us up all night," Thridi said.

"And we're to give over our room to the troll and her babe," Annar told him.

"Can't be out in the sun or she'll turn to stone."

"So we've had nah chance to break our fast."

"It's been all fast and nah break, you could say."

"Or you could just say we're hungry."

"Ravenous."

"Hungry as Huldra."

"And we all know how that ends!"

"How do you mean?" Aspen asked, puzzled.

Snail shook her head.

"He doesna know," said Thridi, turning to his brother.

"He slept through the pother," Annar added.

Triumphantly, they said together, "The troll ate the spy!"

"Look out, teeth, take care gums," Annar said.

"Down the gullet, here he comes," Thridi finished.

"Shut up!" Snail glared at the two of them. "You've big mouths for little folk!"

Aspen gulped. "Why did the professor not stop her?"

The dwarfs giggled. It was a high chittering sound.

"The professor *told* her to do it. Said we couldn't very well travel with a dead body; tossing it somewhere would make the discovery inevitable." Annar grinned. "Do you like that word, brother?"

"Inevitably," Thridi replied.

"He said we didn't have the time or energy to bury the

man. Besides, you couldn't hunt for Huldra anymore, so he gave her a direct order to eat up, and make it quick," Annar said.

"He went down headfirst," Thridi added. "In case you wanted to know."

Aspen felt sick and suddenly understood why Snail had looked so blanched and pale. The troll had eaten the cloaked man after all, and Odds was clearly not what he seemed.

The sooner we get out of here, the better.

He managed to control his face, but just. *How do we do it?*

He wondered about that for a moment, and then suddenly had a plan.

"You could have dinner now," he said, "or breakfast. Snail and I will watch the unicorns for a bit."

The brothers looked at each other and quickly came to an unspoken agreement. Annar handed the reins to Snail and they both jumped past Aspen, who was scrambling up to the driver's perch.

"Back in two shakes of a bear's tail," Annar said.

Aspen knew what was expected. "Bears do not have tails," he said.

Thridi winked at him. "We'll be twice as quick, then!"

The dwarfs disappeared into the wagon and Aspen sat down next to Snail.

"We could leave now," he whispered.

She looked at him sharply. "Don't be ridiculous. We can't wander around in the dark. Annar says we'll reach town by midday and they'll be doing a show. We can sneak out during it." She gasped. "Oh, but what about Huldra and Og? We can't leave them with Odds."

"You *must* be joking!" he said.

"I brought that baby into the world and . . ."

"You were fine before with leaving them here."

"That was before I remembered my oath."

He was puzzled. "Your oath?"

"My midwife's oath."

"Oh that!"

She gave him another of her glares. "So a midwife's oath is worth less than a prince's?"

"Well, of course it is."

"Isn't!"

"Is!"

Of a sudden, he realized they were squabbling like drows in a nest. He was glad the unicorns didn't seem to need any direction to stay on the weedy track that passed for a road, because Snail was paying *no* attention to them at all.

"We may *have* to leave them, oath or not," he said. "We cannot feed them, and they certainly cannot hide very well."

"But Odds might kill them."

"We do not know that. But I fear we have done all we can for them and must look to our own safety now." He glanced at the reins in Snail's hands and then up ahead to where the road curved. "And I still think we should leave now."

"Why? It makes no sense to leave now."

"Well, Odds has cast me in the play. So we will not be able to sneak out during it."

Snail shrugged. "Then we'll sneak out after the play." She blinked twice rapidly. "Wait! The play is *Eal, Ollm, and Fydir*, right?"

Aspen nodded.

"And you're in it?"

He nodded again.

"Hrmmm, you're right. We may need to sneak out earlier. You onstage as a prince might make you entirely too recognizable." Suddenly, she slammed her fist holding the reins on the seat beside them. The unicorns jumped nervously in their harnesses as the reins tightened unexpectedly. "How could Odds do that?"

"Yes, um . . . exactly." He reached for the reins. "Maybe I should . . ."

She yanked the reins away from him and half the unicorns leaned left while the others leaned right. "Wait a moment! Odds didn't cast you as the prince, did he? He's far too clever for that."

Aspen could feel his face turning red. "Um . . . no. Dagmarra has the honor of that role."

"As well she should. She's both *honest* and *brave*. Both princely traits, don't you think?"

"Yes. And I aspire to them as well, but . . ."

Snail was smiling at him now. But it wasn't a particularly

nice smile. "He didn't cast you as the dragon, either, did he?"

Aspen shook his head miserably.

Snail gave a short bark of laughter. "Having to play the princess is no reason for us to risk our lives by sneaking out of here at night with no plan, no supplies, and no real chance of escape if Odds decides to try to track us down."

Aspen nodded mutely. She was right in every particular and he felt a total cad for having tried to talk her into leaving early to avoid his embarrassment.

"At least you'll be able to dress according to your station again."

He stopped reaching for the reins and looked at her. "Odds said the same thing to me last night."

As soon as the words were out of his mouth, he wanted to put them back in. Snail was staring at him agape, sure that he was insinuating that she was like the professor, whereas he was truly only observing the fact that the professor had said the same thing last night. Aspen was afraid that she would strike at him with the reins in her hand, thereby sending the wagon over onto its side.

"Wait, I—" he began, but could not finish, because the dwarfs chose that moment to reappear and clamber neatly up onto the seat beside them.

"Thank you, skarm drema," Annar said to Snail, deftly plucking the reins from her hand and calming the unicorns with a click of his tongue and a few soft twitches on the reins.

"And thank you, Princess Eal," Thridi said. "Without the memory of your beauty . . ."

"Your grace," Annar said.

"Your charm."

"Your *Serenity*."

Both dwarfs paused and bowed to Aspen in their seats.

"We'd not have made it through our trials," Annar said.

"And by trials, we mean our meal."

"The meat was quite tough."

"Bound to repeat on us," Thridi said, pounding on his chest.

"Might want to get below."

"Meat?" said Snail, looking appalled.

"Just a phrase," said Thridi.

"A phase," Annar added.

"A joke."

"Not that bloke."

The twins looked at each other and laughed.

"Actually," Thridi said, "it was a couple of chicken thighs from the last old rooster."

"Roasted."

"Repasted."

"And now repeating," said Thridi.

Aspen sighed. "I guess I had better go," he told them. "I really *do* have lines to learn."

He tried to catch Snail's eye as he was climbing down, but she was studiously avoiding looking at him.

❖ ❖ ❖

LIMPING BACK TO the twins' room, Aspen found the script where he'd left it on the floor. He shuffled through it, picking out Eal's lines and repeating them softly to himself. They were as gaudy and bright as the dress he was expected to wear. And as silly. He wondered that the lines had never seemed that way to him before. But then he had never had to recite them.

> Oh prince of my heart,
> Let us not part . . .

Eal's and Fydir's lines were no better, but at least they would be dressed appropriately.

And not just for their station.

He shuddered at the sudden thought of what Maggie Light might be planning to do with his hair.

"This is going to be a disaster," he said to the bowser when it slinked partway onto his lap for its customary scratching.

Aspen had no idea then how right he was.

SNAIL FIRST SEES THE FAIR

*L*ong before the dawn, Huldra, with Og in her arms, climbed into the wagon to sleep the day away.

No one remarked on how low the wagon sank down on its wheels. No one had to. The unicorns strained more than before, but they didn't complain either. They just hunched their shoulders, gave a hough or two, then responded to the light tap of the reins on their hindquarters and pulled the wagon forward without any noticeable lag.

Snail knew that no horse, not even a heavy Unseelie warhorse, could have pulled as well as a unicorn. And the team seemed to move as one—one mind, one will, one great magic-filled muscle.

As the wagon rolled into the dawn, the sun rose over the eastern hills, almost in their eyes.

Once the three dwarfs came out again, they'd totally taken over the handling of the reins, but as always, they were not loathe to share their knowledge.

Though, Snail thought, *you have to sift through the silliness and the jokes to find it.*

When she'd asked how far it was to the fairgrounds, Annar had said, "Fair enough." And Thridi had added that asking was fair game.

"Speak plain!" Dagmarra said as she pushed past Snail. Taking her place in between the dwarfs, she cuffed both her brothers on the back of the head.

It was not a soft tap and Annar made the sound of a rabbit screaming, then said, "We'll be there by midday."

"It should have been earlier," Annar added, rubbing his head, all humor gone, "if Dagmarra's girlfriend had been a bit lighter."

"But she canna be lighter," retorted Thridi, "for she's a troll and to be in the light would turn her into stone. And stone is not lighter, but heavier."

That returned Annar to his good humor, and he giggled and slapped his brother's hand. "Good 'un!" he crowed.

Snail groaned. It didn't seem such a good 'un to her.

❖ ❖ ❖

THE WAGON PASSED through seven small woods where thrushes sang from the trees, a lovely concert that accompanied them for miles.

"The Seven Sisters," Annar said as they went along the edge of the fifth forest. "There's a story about them, but it's slipped my mind. Something about the Border Lords and marriages and . . ."

Thridi grinned. "Yer mind's always slippery."

"It's greased with ideas," Annar replied.

"I think I know that tale," Dagmarra said. "It doesn't end happily."

Snail thought, *Stories about the Border Lords seldom do.* Even with the sun warming her face, and all the birds in chorus around the wagon, her mood was grim.

Wood squirrels red as trillium ran across the path and in between the unicorns' legs, never getting trodden upon, which surprised Snail. A lazy green snake fell onto the dwarfs' platform from one of the trees. Annar made a strange sound and drew up his legs, but Thridi picked up the snake, which curled its tail around his wrist until he flicked it into the undergrowth.

Around midmorning Aspen reappeared and climbed back up, squeezing past Dagmarra to sit next to Snail.

She tried a smile on, saying, "Do you have your lines?"

He nodded, answering, "I believe so, such as they are." He turned to Annar. "How far now?"

Annar grunted, perhaps finally tired enough to subdue his chattiness. "We'll be there by midday."

They seemed in no hurry, and Snail said something about it, wondering—with war about to break over them like a great wave—why they were trundling along as if they'd all the time in the world.

Dagmarra answered before her brothers could make their jokes. "The beasts will pull all day and all night, but nothing will cause them to run," she said, "except maybe a hungry lion or troll nipping at their heels!"

"Well, we have one of those at least," Snail said, but under her breath so no one heard.

❖ ❖ ❖

THE ROAD SEEMED to go on for so long, and the day was so soft and sunny, that everyone but Annar was dozing on the perch. But after one long, lazy turn, they came over a small hill, and Snail woke with a start because Annar had cried out, "There it is!"

At first all Snail saw were the backs of the unicorns, their muscles bunched and straining, wet with unicorn sweat, which was pink and smelled like roses.

But as they started down, soon enough she could make out a middling town of winding streets and, in the large green meadow on its western flank, a series of stalls under bright canopies with red and gold banners flapping and snapping in a steady lowland breeze.

She tried counting the stalls, stopped at forty.

Dagmarra crowed. "Bogborough. Good town, good day, good market, good crowd. The professor had worried that with the threat of the Border Lords and the Unseelie hordes, people would have stayed at home. Boarding up their windows. Hiding their animals. Carting water from their wells. But maybe they're here to stock up on provisions before any battle."

"*Well, well, well,*" Annar said.

"Indeed, we should do *well* enough," added Thridi.

"Welcome," they said together, and giggled.

Dagmarra just gave them a look that seemed a bit disgusted and a bit amused.

"Where do we set up?" asked Aspen, just as if he and Snail weren't planning to run off before the play. Or after it. Or during it. She didn't remember what they'd actually agreed on the timing—or how they were to go.

We're going to have to talk again—and soon, Snail thought, remembering how swiftly their planning turned into squabbling last night. *Though we're much better at leaving than talking about it.*

She understood why Aspen was asking about setting up. Whether they were leaving before, during, or after the play, they both had to act as if running away was the last thing on their minds. They had to make everyone believe that the fair was so enticing that they couldn't wait to help with the show.

Annar pointed to the far left side of the meadow. "There," he said. "Flat ground, away from the bog and away from the hurly of the stalls but close enough to entice them to our stage."

"Our *stage?*" Snail asked.

"Just wait," Thridi answered.

Which of course she had to do.

❖ ❖ ❖

As THEY GOT closer, everything came into focus as if Snail was now looking through a wizard's scry. The banners were not just red and gold but had the Seelie king's insignia emblazoned on both sides.

"Means they're sanctioned by the throne," whispered Aspen.

Snail suddenly feared that would also mean there would be the king's guard there to watch over the site. And indeed, just as she had that thought, a small company of soldiers came around a bunch of houses and began to make their way toward the wagon.

"Inside!" Dagmarra said to Snail and Aspen, and without arguing, they scrambled in before they could be seen.

Once hidden, Aspen turned on Snail and hissed, "I told you we should have left before. Now we are surrounded by soldiers."

She glared at him. "I wasn't the one who brought them here." When he said nothing, she went on. "We stick with the plan."

"What plan?"

He's right for once, she thought. *We don't really have a plan. Just a notion, an idea, a wish, a dream.*

She said quickly, "You perform the play. I gather supplies. We leave in the night."

He snorted, whether at the plan or the thought of his part in the play she didn't know. Either way, it infuriated her.

"I'm going into Maggie's room," she told him. "It's probably safest there." She was already past Huldra, who was sleeping on the floor next to Dagmarra's bed, with Og drooling mightily in her arms.

"Then I will come with you," Aspen said in a loud whisper.

She wanted to turn and say, "Don't you dare," but the wagon suddenly stopped short, and they were both thrown onto the floor, Aspen coming to a stop close to the troll's head.

And a bit too close to her open mouth, thought Snail frantically as she tumbled by. She ended partway into the next room, where the golden bowser growled in her direction and showed its many teeth.

As she lay there, checking her body parts and realizing she wasn't actually hurt, Snail wondered what to do next. She heard Dagmarra call loudly, "Halloo, soldiers, come to help us set up? Tonight Professor Odds's players will perform *Eal, Ollm, and Fydir* as you have never seen it before. The dragon will be a revelation."

"It snorts," said Annar, equally loudly.

"It blows fire and smoke," added Thridi. He, too, was all but shouting.

"It flies!" the three dwarfs shouted together.

Snail realized they were talking that way to inform Aspen and herself of what was happening. She sat back on her heels and listened to the rest.

Presumably it was the captain of the guard who answered. "We will not help you set up. We have to be alert for Unseelie folk. But we *will* get to watch the dragon fly." And then, as if an afterthought, he spoke two of the dragon's lines:

> I bluster, I fester, I blow,
> and down your castle will go!

At that, Aspen sat up and whispered, "My brother taught me those lines. Do you suppose . . ."

But Snail whispered back, "No supposing. And no looking out the door to check, either. We need to stay hidden and get away as soon as we can."

"*Before* the play?" he said, all of a sudden looking happy.

She had to suppress the urge to slap him. "Sure, because *that's* what's important here: you not wanting to perform."

"Well, someone could recognize me . . ."

"Or *laugh* at you," she said, "and that would be a tragedy!" She stood up and spun on her heel, making her way through the door into Maggie Light's room as if only there could she be safe.

"Well of course they will laugh," he said, his face fixed in a pout. "We have had no time to rehearse. I have not spoken to the director—whoever that may be. And it will be my

first time ever on a stage. If Odds wants me to be incon-
spicuous, he has certainly taken an odd way to show it."

Odd indeed, she agreed silently, and closed the door before
Aspen could follow. She would have locked it had there been
a key. *At least I'll be alone here for a while,* she thought. *His
pride will keep him out if nothing else.*

She was perched on Maggie Light's bed for only a few
moments before Professor Odds found her.

"You've no part in the play," he said, "but you still have a
part to play." He reached out his hand to her.

She wished for once that he'd just come out and say what
he meant. Then she revised that thought: *Maybe I* don't
want to know what he means.

In fact, all she wanted to do was leave. Leave with Aspen,
she realized—no matter that she was mad at him right now.
Leave and get away from this crazy professor, his murderous
assistant, his talking bird and his double-talking dwarfs, his
growling rug . . .

She briefly considered kicking Odds in the shin and making a run for it, but that would leave Aspen and Huldra and
Og behind. And she couldn't do that.

Besides, she thought, *the wagon is still surrounded by
soldiers.*

So, she ignored the professor's hand but—acting as if she
was in his thrall—followed him from the room.

ASPEN DRESSES UP

*A*spen had heard Odds speaking to Snail through the closed door and realized that she was fine, but he did not go in. The old professor gave him the willies, and he had to figure out when and how he and Snail might get away.

The wagon began moving again, making strange creaking and groaning sounds. *Rather like a troll in labor*, he thought—remembering the time in the troll's cave where he had assisted Snail when Huldra gave birth to Og. He was wondering how long and how far they had to go into the fairgrounds, when the wagon slowed and then stopped again.

The groaning and creaking ceased and all was quiet.

For about three minutes.

Then a horrendous scraping sound began over his head. Aspen was briefly afraid a roc had traveled from the western wastes all the way through Unseelie territory and across the Unmastered Lands just to tear the roof off the wagon. Of course he had never actually seen a roc, though his tutor Jaunty had told him all about them. But surely if there had been a roc, there would be screaming coming from the crowd in the meadow, who were strangely silent, except for an occasional "oooh!" and "aaah!"

Despite the creaking, grumbling, scraping noises, the roof didn't seem to have moved, and the sound was soon over.

Then Aspen heard Annar and Thridi shouting outside. Since it sounded like instructions and not at all like a full-on panic, he stayed put.

Another scraping started, this time under his feet.

Next there was banging and clanging and the wagon shook and swayed as if they were moving again. But oddly, there was no sense of forward motion.

"*Oddly,*" he thought. *Everything about Professor Odds and his crew can be summed up in some form of that one word.* Still he waited.

At last, though, his curiosity got the better of his sense of caution. *Soldiers or no soldiers, I have to know what is happening.*

He supposed he could peek out the back door, but then he would be running the risk of being spotted. Suddenly, he remembered that Snail had told him of a spyhole in Maggie Light's room. He could peer out of that with no danger at all.

If he could find it. And if Snail and the professor were no longer there.

The professor was always a problem!

Aspen also worried about running into the dwarfs, whose

room he had to go through to get to Maggie Light's. But surely they were still outside. He listened but could not hear any more shouts. It was a gamble he was willing to take.

Besides, he told himself, *Dagmarra had only said to get inside, not to stay in any one room in the wagon.*

A part of him hoped he would run into Maggie Light.

Moving quietly, he got to the door, where he listened intently but heard nothing. The racket from outside had ceased.

Pushing the door open just a crack, he peeked through. When he saw what was on the other side, he gasped and involuntarily pushed it fully open.

The dwarfs' room was just *gone.* As was Maggie Light's. Or rather, their left walls were gone, and the beds and sparse furnishings were just now being hidden behind a lowering tan curtain. What was left of the rooms were now open to a field of long grasses where several groups of fey children tumbled and played while a small knot of mothers—mostly brownies and low-caste elves—looked on.

A walkway extended from the wagon ten paces into the field, and the ceiling canted up and away. The wall between the rooms was disappearing as well, being lifted up by what at first appeared to be a gigantic silver spider that groaned and creaked as it worked.

He shuddered. He had never liked spiders and this one was almost as large as the wagon. Only then did he realize with a start that the spider was not alive but was instead some kind of made being, its legs of cold iron, which meant that no one of Faerie but dwarfs could have had a hand in the making of it. Cold iron burned any other fey straight through to the bone.

As he watched further, the spider drew a deep blue curtain across the more ordinary curtain to make a back wall.

Now he understood what had happened. The central part of the wagon had been turned into a stage. The wonder was that it had taken him so long to figure it out.

For just a moment, Aspen thought that a giant stood at the front of this new stage until he realized that it was really the three dwarfs standing on one another's shoulders. Annar was on top, fastening the last of a dozen screened lanterns along the outer edge of the now-slanted ceiling. That done, he began tying the screens to a complicated system of ropes that led to the side of the wagon, ropes that snaked down the wall and into the professor's room.

"Oh!" Aspen said aloud.

Hearing Aspen's gasp, Dagmarra—who was on the bottom, holding up her brothers—turned, ignoring Annar's squeals of protest. Thridi in the middle just looked pained.

"Hauld yer whist!" she admonished. "Are ye daft? Get yerself inside. And don't come back out until yer dressed a proper princess!"

She seemed angry enough to let both her brothers fall so that she could come and punch Aspen, so he hurriedly shut the door and shuffled back into the twins' room. He thought briefly about leaving now while everyone was busy.

I could just walk out the back door and disappear and no one would know I was gone until Maggie Light came to dress me.

But it would mean leaving without Snail. And somehow that was not possible.

Might as well get ready for the play, then.

❖ ❖ ❖

BY THE TIME Maggie Light came to help him into his costume, Aspen was already in the dress, but it was pulled over his traveling clothes, which made him look like a rather hefty and lumpy princess. He thought he could use his dagger to cut the dress away in a matter of moments when they were ready to make their escape.

And I must admit, I am quite looking forward to cutting this dreadful garment to bits.

Still, he could not help feeling warm when Maggie Light oohed and aahed over how he looked and told him how well he'd done in buttoning, lacing, tying, and cinching the dress up.

He admitted it had not been easy. "Truly, it is a wonder a woman ever leaves the house with the preparation it takes."

Maggie Light nodded in agreement. "And we're not half done, either."

"What?"

"There's the makeup and the wig and the shoes, still."

"Oh," he said, staring down at his stockinged feet. He had not considered those things at all.

I remember when I used to like getting dressed up. In men's clothes, of course, but still . . .

With all that he had experienced lately, the blood, the death, the betrayal—*and the friendship, bravery, and sacrifice* he reminded himself, thinking of Snail—he was certain he could never again enjoy the frivolous pastimes of his youth. Then he smiled. *Pretty deep thoughts for a prince in a dress.*

"You seem happy about the play," Maggie Light said. "That's good!"

He swallowed the sigh he felt rising, and let Maggie Light pin his hair up and start applying some kind of noxious powder to his face. All the while, he worked hard at making no complaints at all.

❖ ❖ ❖

SOME TIME PASSED before he was completely transformed into Princess Eal. Maggie Light held a mirror in front of his face. Reflected in the glass was a garish trollop, with the emphasis on the *troll*.

"Um," he said, trying to think of something positive to say and failing utterly.

"Stage makeup," Maggie Light said by way of explanation. "It will look much better from far away."

Aspen stared at his reflection critically. "Will they be

watching from Trollholm?" That was the kingdom of the creatures, sung of in ballads, though no one, Aspen mused, had ever returned to tell the truth of it.

Maggie Light gave her bell-like laugh. "That might not be far enough."

Aspen stood unsteadily in the princess's high shoes. "Well, I guess I can play it strictly for laughs."

"That's how we like it played," Maggie Light said, "and you'll be playing it soon."

"Is it time?"

"Peek through the door." She opened it a crack.

Aspen peeked through and saw that it was already early evening. His stomach began to growl. He had no idea when he had last eaten. But his stomach was also roiling with fear. And then the fear filled his mouth like a foul liquid. He knew it was not fear of the soldiers. He had hardly given them a thought. It was fear of going out onto the stage and playing to that huge crowd.

Screened lanterns had been lit, and the giant spider, with its metal legs, was pulling on the ropes, shifting the screens back and forth. Streams of colored light in blues and reds and greens, and colors Aspen did not even know the names of, spilled from the lanterns onto the stage to fight with the amber light from the setting sun. The meadow grass had been trampled into a flat expanse by the rollicking children, and dozens of audience members already stood on the cleared ground. Some were watching the stage lights, others just gossiping or telling jokes.

Maggie put two fingers into her mouth and gave out an enormous whistle. The spider folded itself down into a box about the size of a valise, the metal legs on the inside. As soon as it was done, Maggie Light strode out onto the stage to huge applause. She waved to the crowd, then picked up the box and, seemingly without struggling with the weight of it, glided back behind the curtain.

Her performance not only pleased the crowd, it startled Aspen so much, he was lost for comment. But as he looked through the door, he could see even more folk walking up from the cook tents a short distance away. At that rate, the field in front of the stage would be full soon.

"Were we expecting this . . ." Aspen found himself gulping. "This big crowd?"

"Oh, yes," Maggie Light said happily. "And it will soon be bigger. You're not frightened, are you?"

He wanted to say no, but suddenly realized that he was more frightened now than when he had been facing execution in his father's court. For some reason he could not lie to her.

"Terrified."

She nodded. "It will fade."

"When?"

Maggie Light smiled with a warmth that belied the cruelty

of her next words. "I've never heard an actor complaining of it past their hundredth performance. Now remember to speak high, in falsetto, so you sound like a girl."

She patted him on the shoulder and left him with his stage fright, his dress, and his now seemingly useless plans for escape.

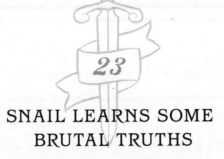

SNAIL LEARNS SOME
BRUTAL TRUTHS

*W*hen Snail and Odds had settled in his room, he'd gestured her to a small chair. She sat and started to protest, but he waved a hand to silence her. Then he reached out to a kind of bellpull by the side of his desk and gave it a yank, which seemed to start a bunch of creaks and groans in motion.

Alarmed, Snail asked, "What's that?"

"Setting the stage," Odds said mysteriously. "Stage craft and craftiness. All in a night's work."

She nodded as if she understood what he meant, but as the creaks and shouts and groans went on, she actually figured it out. She'd seen such a thing before, though never on such a grand scale. The wagon would be turned into the players' stage.

"You said I have a role, sir . . ." she began.

He sat down in his big chair, which made him tower over her. "You do, indeed." He smiled at her and there was no comfort in it.

Snail waited for him to speak, then waited some more. At last she said, "Is it a secret?"

"It's not, though you seemed unaware of it. However, it's nothing to beware of. It's who you are."

Now she was confused. "I'm Snail, a midwife's apprentice of the Unseelie Court." She stopped. "Or at least I was a few days ago. Now I seem to be an actual midwife in the Seelie lands, running from two armies and . . ."

Odds held up a hand. "And yet none of what you just said is the truth."

"Well, of course it is," she told him, thinking that in fact it was the first time since meeting Odds she *had* told the truth. That he should say otherwise made her furious. She started to glare at him as she stood up.

"Have you never wondered why you were different from the other apprentices? Why your eyes are . . ."

"Two different colors, you mean?"

"Not just that. They aren't the pure blue of the fey folk." He looked at her. "Your hair . . . ?"

"Red."

"No fey has red hair. Your parentage?"

"I was brought up by Mistress Softhands, the midwife and . . ."

He leaned forward, "Not just brought up. In fact, you were adopted as a child, yes? And you're more awkward than your friends, with less magical ability, yet you did that puzzle I set you quickly, which I can assure you none of them could have done."

"I didn't finish it," she admitted, blushing, remembering how she'd put it aside. Almost slammed it down in frustration, actually.

"I saw how quickly you got it undone. With a bit more time . . ." His grey eyes seemed to glitter.

"You were *spying* on me!" Now she really glared.

"Of course," he said, less an admission than a boast.

"But . . ." She sat down heavily in the chair again.

"But me no buts, and butter me no bread," he said. "I'll not give you an oily answer but a plain one. Have you looked at your fingers?"

She sighed. "Even when you say you're going to speak plainly, you riddle, Professor Odds."

"Look at your fingers," he repeated. "Your middle finger is longer than the rest. Yet a fey has hands where all the fingers except the thumb are the same height."

She bit her lip. She knew that was true but had thought it only strange, not something that defined her.

"You're skarm drema, child. A human girl, stolen by the fey to do their bidding and to be used eventually as a tithe to their dark gods."

She wanted to tell him he was wrong. She was fey, she knew she was. Why, she could even do a few small spells. But, oddly she couldn't argue with him, because—as if a burning torch had just illuminated her life—everything suddenly made a kind of sense.

Only not entirely.

"A human child?" she breathed, not quite believing it.

He nodded.

She leaned forward and said shortly, "Then who are my parents?"

"That I don't know."

"Then how do you know they're human?"

"Because *you* clearly are."

"Can I find them?"

"No. It's not possible."

"Why not?" This time when she stood up, she began to pace in front of him. "If the fey brought humans here, surely there is a door back into the human world? A gate? A crossing place?"

Odds didn't answer, but she could see the answer in his eyes.

"There is, isn't there?" she said, almost begging.

This time he nodded.

"Show it to me."

"It doesn't matter. Entering from this side will age you beyond your years before you even land in the human plane." He shook his head. "And it's not always open. Only on the blue moon."

Now she knew he was lying, had been lying all along. But

why? But instead of tasking him with it, she sneered. "The *blue* moon? I've never *heard* of a blue moon. Or seen one. Moons are yellow or gold or, once in a while, orange."

"That's because they're not actually blue and only occur as the third full moon in a month of four."

"Then why call it blue?"

"A human conceit," he admitted. "And being human, not always understandable."

She remembered the other word he'd used. "Month? What is a month?" She was totally at sea now.

"It's the human way of counting days in a season," he said. "They have four seasons: spring, summer, winter, autumn."

"Only four of them?"

"Only four."

Snail thought four a paltry number. The fey seasons were nine in all: Springtide, River Spate, Rosebay, Trout Rise, Berrybreak, Leafmeal, Hailstone, Snowfall, each ending in a Solstice celebration. And of course the moveable season of Change, which came and went in a rhythm only wizards fully understood. How could there be only *four* seasons? It made human life a small, stunted thing. She didn't want to be human. She was fey. She'd always been fey.

She said so, and Odds laughed.

"Humans are smart, cunning, inventive," he said. "They're the storytellers and clock makers, playwrights and poets. Without them, the universe would be a less interesting place."

She had no idea what a universe was, but remembered

what she'd been taught by her mentor, Mistress Softhands, and told Odds. "Humans are useless, puling, short-lived, ugly, a rough copy of the fey," she said angrily. "They live hard, die young. I'd *know* if I were human!"

He stood up all at once, looking very tall, very powerful. Like a wizard, she thought suddenly, fear a heavy stone in her belly.

"*I* am human, child," he said, his voice suddenly soft. "And you are, too, whether you fully comprehend that or not. What I'm about—what you *need* to be about—is saving all those human children who over the years have been stolen, used, abused, kept in slavery by the wicked fey. What *skarm drema* truly means is 'freedom for the slaves.'"

Snail burst into tears; she wasn't sure why.

He waited until she was done sobbing and only snuffling up the last of the nose drips. Then he said, "This is your part to play this evening. You'll go through the crowd and whisper the words *skarm drema*. To those who answer *drema skarm*, you will hand one of these special tickets." He gave her a packet of greenish cards. "Only a human will be able to make out the writing, which is a map to our meeting six days hence. And there, we will lay our plans to finally become free."

"But . . ."

"But me no buts. You owe it to the other humans, to your human parents, to yourself."

The cards felt cold in her hand. They felt like a ticket to

a foreign place. To a world in which the seasons were four and the people, though walking about, were dead. She had no more connection to that world than to the Unseelie kingdom, which had played her false and was now trying to find and kill her. Nor did she owe any allegiance to the Seelie kingdom, which was doing the very same thing. She'd thought she'd found a home with the professor and his players, but that, too, had turned out to be false.

Still, she had to make the professor think she'd accepted this new role until she could figure out her way through all that he'd just told her and plan her escape.

"Now, take this cloak and wrap it about you. Then go out into the audience. Keep your focus on the people who look a bit odd, a bit out of place, not the brownies or the hobs, not the trolls or the little people. You'll know the human folk. They'll be the oddest of all. More importantly, they'll know you."

"I thought you said that the changelings were all slaves."

"These are the brave ones who've made their way out of the Unseelie lands, along the night paths to freedom. Or bought their way across the water to the freer lands of the Seelie folk, where they have used their gifts to make themselves a better life."

Odds said this as if it were a speech he'd given before. But it was all new to Snail, and she had many more questions to put to him.

"But professor . . . "

He put up a hand to stop her. "No more time for talk."

She stood, put on the cloak, let him push her out of the door. Anything to get away from him and the geas he'd laid on her, that magical proscription, the *skarm drema* spell.

Walking outside into the waiting crowd, she whispered to herself, "I'm *not* human. I *won't* be human. I *can't* be human."

The people in the audience ignored her mutterings. They only had eyes for the stage. Mouths agape like frogs, they stared straight ahead.

Snail couldn't help herself. She turned and watched the stage as well, just as Aspen came out, looking as miserable as she felt.

When he opened his mouth to say his first words, he seemed to freeze. She knew the opening speech, could have shouted it out to him.

I am and am not the Princess Eal.
And none of you knows how I feel.
For I've been stolen for to slave
Inside a dragon's dark, jeweled cave . . .

For the first time, the words struck her, as hard as the force of a troll's cudgel. If Odds was to be believed, and humans were the storytellers and poets, then a human had written the play about Princess Eal.

"Skarm drema!" she whispered. "'For I've been stolen for to slave inside a dragon's dark, jeweled cave . . .'"

By her left side, a woman with orange hair and a turned-up nose looked at her, not at all startled, and whispered back, "Drema skarm. Time to leave the cave, sister."

Without questioning it further, Snail handed her one of the cards.

24

ASPEN PLAYS HIS PART

The sun went down, the stage lights went up, and Maggie Light pushed Aspen onto the stage. Where he immediately forgot his first line.

Instead, he was mesmerized by the multitude of faces in the audience: elven soldiers, lower-caste fey, mud-folk peasants, the odd middle-class merchant or laird come to the fair for a bit of low entertainment. They all shared a certain expectant look, as if they believed they might actually be about to see a magical world where brave princes fought mighty dragons to rescue beautiful princesses, though of course everyone knew that dragons no longer existed. Except in stories. Or plays. Or the occasional song.

He supposed that once upon a time, he'd looked at the stage like that: mouth agape, expecting magic.

But there will be no magic tonight, folks, he thought bitterly. *It is all colored lights, ropes, and a whole lot of bad acting. A prince in a dress, a dwarf dressed as a prince.*

He looked out at the faces of the shopkeepers, farmers,

day laborers, and other menials who did the actual work of his father's kingdom and thought about the tiny magicks they wielded. He even saw Snail making her way through the crowd, a magicless, lower-class girl.

But braver than any prince I have ever known.

He included himself in that number.

Suddenly, a trapdoor cleverly concealed in the grains of the wooden floor popped open in front of him. It was only a crack, but as if to prove how much braver Snail was than he, he nearly startled right out of his massive costume.

First a nose and then a beard poked out of the trapdoor and Annar hissed, *"I am and am not the Princess Eal."*

"Oh, yes. Right." He cleared his throat, looked over at the audience, and began.

> I am and am not the Princess Eal.
> And none of you knows how I feel.
> For I've been stolen for to slave
> Inside a dragon's dark, jeweled cave . . .

That was not half bad, he thought, before looking back at the onlookers. They stared aghast and he suddenly realized that he hadn't spoken in a falsetto, as Maggie had reminded him to, but instead had used his normal—and quite male—voice.

Oh. No.

He tried to redo the lines in a girl's voice, but squeaked

the first line and coughed on the second and, to his eternal horror, the crowd started laughing. He stopped before repeating the third line, and tried on a smile.

Maybe we can *play this thing for laughs.*

Then he turned to see Dagmarra making her entrance. She looked every inch the brave and martial prince, though those inches were rather few.

And she was staring daggers right at Aspen.

So, he thought miserably, *we shall* not *be playing this for humor.*

With a great deal of emotion—and, Aspen had to admit, a fair amount of thespian skill—Dagmarra began to deliver her lines:

> I am Ollm and Ollm I am,
> Prince of fey and beast and man.
> With sword and shield and magicks, too,
> I have come to rescue . . .

But neither Aspen nor the crowd got to hear what Dagmarra was going to do with her sword and shield and magicks, because just then one of the soldiers in the crowd let out a howling scream.

There was a black arrow sticking out from under his arm, the one place the breastplate did not protect. He pawed at it ineffectually for a moment and then fell. There was the briefest bit of silence, as the crowd tried to figure out whether this was part of the play or not. But when more arrows flew into the crowd, hitting soldier and peasant alike, everyone began screaming.

Snail! Aspen thought.

He looked over to where he had seen her last, but the crowd was stampeding now, the night closing in, and it was impossible to make out one small redheaded girl in the bubbling ocean of frightened folk.

What he *did* see were fell creatures wading into the crowd now, black and green, with too many teeth and not enough limbs. But what limbs they did have were clawed or taloned or holding black knives. More creatures followed behind them, warty and short, and tall and hairy, and dark and smoky, as if they were only halfway here in this world. He knew them of course. They were drows and boggarts and bogles and bogies. They were leshies and lycants, kelpies, and members of the Wild Hunt.

"Unseelie!" someone shouted. Aspen thought it might have been him.

And I'm standing onstage in a dress.

Arrows thunked into the stage now, and Aspen drew his dagger from the folds of the dress. He thought about cutting the costume off with it, rubbing his face free of the woman's makeup, but realized there was no time. He would have to fight as he was.

"But not in these shoes!" He realized belatedly that he

had shouted the lines as he kicked off the silly things and dove off the stage.

Seelie folk were desperately running this way and that, not sure of where the attacks were coming from or which way to go to get away. Some of them had fallen and were being trampled by friend and foe alike.

Aspen thought he might be trampled as well, but he began a swimming motion that pushed people away from him while moving him through the crowd. He felt hobbled by the dress and hated it, but he kept going, glad the shoes at least were gone.

Once, he had to stop his swimming motion to avoid stabbing a brownie child, and while that was the noble thing to do, he was immediately buffeted, then knocked sideways.

A black-clawed hand swung at his face and he cut at it wildly with his dagger. He must have scored a hit because he heard a squeal and the hand disappeared.

Catching a brief glimpse of a redhead that he thought might be Snail, he tried to push toward her, but the sheer press of people was carrying him along now. He was a piece of driftwood with its hair standing on end.

With its hair standing on end?

CRAAAAACK!

Aspen was blinded by a blue light as the smell of lightning and burnt flesh filled the air. He and the crowd members nearest him filled the air, too, unaccountably lifted up and flung back toward the stage. They landed in a heap of broken limbs and bleeding skulls. Aspen hit the ground and then desperately kept rolling because his dress had caught fire from the lightning spell.

I guess we will *see magic tonight.*

Standing up at last in the burned rags of his costume, head ringing, half-blind in one eye, he found he'd lost his dagger, but at least he was back by the stage, which meant he was out of the crowd a bit.

The lower-castes were still running about mindlessly. They had no idea how to fight a battle.

If someone does not lead them soon, he thought, *it will be a complete slaughter.*

He turned to look up at the stage, all the while thinking, *War should be fought soldier to soldier, not like this. This is the cutting down of cattle; this is simply fish pulled up in nets.*

There were children lying bleeding against the stage, women with red wounds blossoming on their breasts. Farmers and shopkeepers torn in two. The area in front of the stage was running red with a river of blood.

The stories he had loved as a boy, the minstrel songs, the great ballads of both Seelie and Unseelie kings, all celebrated heroism and heroic deaths in battle. Even the Border Lords came back from raids joking about their scars.

But this, Aspen thought, *no one ever sings about* this. *No tales talk of such destruction on the large scale or the small.*

Meanwhile, the Seelie soldiers were trying to recover, but they were badly outnumbered. As they called out to one another to regroup, to find their leaders, the black and green Unseelie monsters were being reinforced by Border Lords in their plaids, swinging huge swords that cut down anything near them: men, women, brownies, selchies, hobs, children. The children, he thought, were the hardest to bear. Why had he never thought of children in war?

He looked at the Border Lords, in their orderly lines. *Like bloody farmers scything the crops,* he thought. *They may be berserkers, but they are disciplined ones. No one will escape this harvesting.* He shuddered.

One of the Seelie officers, of obvious noble blood, was trying desperately to rally his troops by flinging spells wildly, hitting friend and foe alike.

Aspen could feel the magic calling to his own, and he felt a rage rising inside him. He tried to suppress it, hold it in. Using his princely magic would alert every wizard in two kingdoms where he was. But here, whatever he thought of it, was true battle. The magic would not be denied.

Blood calls to blood, as the old Seelie saying went. His blood, his noble blood, was being called out.

"I am the Bright Celestial!" he shouted, barely able to keep from naming himself. "I am Ruire of the Tir na nOg!" He raised his empty hands and saw that they were ringed with fire. "And you shall regret interrupting my performance!"

The magic exploded from him, shooting flames from his fingertips. It washed into a row of kelpies and they screamed and withered to ash and crumbling seaweed.

A dozen Border Lord archers notched arrows and turned to face this new threat. The remaining kelpies nickered and neighed as they swung away from the fleeing crowd to surround Aspen.

They have, he thought wildly, *very sharp teeth for horses.*

Boggarts howled, drows made a jubilant ululating sound. The lycants growled so loudly, it sounded like thunder. Aspen managed—but only just—to keep from putting his fingers in his ears.

Not far from the stage came the sound of goblins in the bushes. *Probably mixing something explosive,* Aspen thought. *Perhaps that war cry was not my best idea ever.* But even as he thought that, he knew it was not something he had chosen to do: Blood called to blood.

Gathering flames around him, a shield and a weapon as one, he prepared to charge to his certain—though quite princely—doom.

But at that very moment, the back of the wagon split open and Huldra—baby Og now strapped to her back—roared out of it, immediately stomping two bogles into the ground. Blood and bones and loosened bowels were ground into the churned-up dirt. She stopped to swallow a third bogle whole, then roared out a belch that shook the ground around her. It would have been funny if it hadn't been so frightening.

A sword was pressed into Aspen's hand and he looked down at three very angry dwarfs holding axes and looking grim.

"Beware!" Dagmarra growled at him, then glanced over her shoulder.

Aspen peered over her shoulder as well.

From behind the wagon came the giant metal spider that had set up the stage. Only this time it was plucking up Border Lords and kelpies, leshies and lycants and tossing them impossibly high into the air. Its legs must have been cold iron because every Unseelie who tried to rush it was burned at the touch. Arrows plinked off the spider's sides as its enemies fell broken onto the ground.

Looking more closely, Aspen saw that the spider carried a strange addition to its iron carapace. Someone was riding the spider as if it were a gigantic steed.

"But that's . . ." Aspen said.

"Odd, isn't it?" Annar pointed out.

Aspen couldn't even smile at the wordplay; there were still enemies before him. And though they were shaken by the sudden appearance of so formidable a foe, they did not look ready to run.

Yet.

Giving a thin grimace to his companions that someone

might mistake for a smile, Aspen turned and fired a gout of flame from his fingers into the ranks of his enemies. Then he followed the flames in, sword at the ready, with Professor Odds's players swooping in from behind to lend him their support.

25

SNAIL MANAGES SOMEHOW

*S*nail didn't see the first arrow or the second, and the first sign she had that the whole evening had changed irrevocably was when she stumbled over a dead Seelie soldier. He was not much older than Aspen, for he hadn't a hint of a beard or the faintest bit of hair on his upper lip. She still didn't understand what was happening until moments later when another soldier fell dead at her feet. Then the screaming began.

Her first thought was of Aspen, then of baby Og, and she turned to run for the wagon. The crowd swept her up and she knew immediately that she wouldn't make it.

The woods! she thought, but they looked impossibly far away. *Well, if I can't run* . . . She drew her knife and looked for someone to fight.

There was no one, just panic and screaming and arrows appearing from the darkness. A girl no older than she stumbled and hit the ground with the sound of a sack of grain being slammed into the dirt. An arrow stuck out of her calf like a serving fork in a solstice hen. Suddenly, Snail felt all doubt fall away.

She threw herself next to the fallen girl, guarding her from the fleeing crowd with her body. The girl was screaming in pain, but the sound was lost among the panicked shouts of the crowd.

However, dealing with screaming women was the *first* thing you learned as a midwife's apprentice.

Snail turned the girl over onto her back, grabbing her leg, and in almost the same motion, knelt on the leg, holding it firm. Unable to sit up, the girl slapped at Snail ineffectually till Snail hissed at her, "Hold still!"

The arrow had gone through the meat of the calf; the bone looked untouched. She slit the girl's leggings, then tore the fabric off in strips.

I'll need those in a moment.

The tip of the arrow was poking out the other side of the girl's leg, but hadn't broken the skin yet. Snail thought briefly about warning the girl what was going to happen next, but didn't think that would help anything.

Grabbing the feathered end of the arrow, she shoved it harshly further into the calf so that the barbed tip sliced through the skin on the far side, and new blood gushed from the wound. She felt the girl struggle, but Snail had her leg secured.

And the leg is all that matters right now.

Snail gave little thought to what she must do, and just did

it. Gone was the midwife's creed: Anticipate, alleviate, and then await. She'd no time for any of that. Do and do and do was her creed now, and worry later about what she'd done or if she'd done enough.

She grabbed the arrow below the tip, careful not to cut herself—hoping it hadn't been dipped in poison—and snapped the tip off. Then she pulled the whole thing back out the way it had gone in, swiftly and smoothly, ignoring the foul names the girl was calling her.

"I'm a trained doctor," she fibbed, but it was like a rag in the girl's mouth, stoppering her insults for the moment.

Grabbing the strips of cloth she'd cut from the leggings, Snail wadded each into the wide punctures in the girl's leg, then tied them tight in place with the rest. Only then did she release her.

The girl glared at her, but her leg was too swollen and bruised for her to move.

"Someone will help you up after a bit," Snail told her. "But at least you are losing no more blood. That's what could have killed you."

And still might, she thought. When women died giving birth it was often due simply to the blood loss. It was one of the first lessons Mistress Softhands had taught. But infection was just as deadly. And she had no herbs to help the girl with that.

A big man in a farmer's tunic was stumbling through the crowd, his nose askew and a brutal gash across the top of his thigh. Blood was waterfalling down his leg. She wasn't sure how he was able to walk with that wound but knew he wouldn't be doing it for much longer—or ever again—if it didn't get tended to soon.

She held up her arms to stop him, but he shook his head and pointed toward the trees. She nodded and followed behind him as he bulled his way through the hordes of people.

The amount of blood seemed to work as a charm, parting the crowd. The farmer collapsed just before the treeline, but there were suddenly hands there to drag him into cover.

Snail cut his pants away from the wound and went to work. At least the farmer didn't curse her, only grunted once or twice. Though like the girl, he gave Snail no thanks for her help. But Snail had been enough times in a birth chamber to know that thanks came only after fear and exhaustion had time to walk out of the room, after the patient was assured of life.

More wounded arrived, some stumbling on their own, some carried. They all came to Snail as if pulled there magically. She examined their wounds, treated those that she could. The others she left to the compassion of the fey gods.

The fey gods, as she knew well, were not always kind.

At one point a woman pressed a needle and thread into her hand, and someone else dried the sweat from her forehead. She realized she had helpers—men who found supplies at her asking, women who dealt with the smaller hurts. She sewed and cut and sweated and at some point she noticed that her own fingers bled from a hundred pin-sticks.

Her shoulders felt like boulders; her back had a permanent ache that ran from one side to the other. But she ignored her own pain as she ignored those wounded who weren't going to die without help, and went back to work. The time seemed to concentrate down to each wound.

After she'd worked on a dozen, two dozen, five dozen . . . maybe even a hundred patients—she'd lost count long ago—the sound of clashing blades and crashing magicks grew dangerously close to her wooded spot. But she had a vein pinched between her fingers, and if she looked away before she closed it, the mother of four lying before her would die in front of her children.

That's not *going to happen!* she promised herself as she stitched the vein and bandaged the wound and no one stuck a sword through her.

Suddenly, there were no more wounded. The woods were dark and relatively quiet, the sounds of war and battle reduced to the whimpering and crying of aftermath.

Either all the Unseelie folk were dead—which was highly unlikely—or they were regrouping elsewhere. Snail stood creakily and looked out into the field where battle had interrupted the play. Bodies were scattered over the trampled grass, most clearly dead, some maybe just dying.

She'd come back and tend them later, but first she had to get to the wagon. She was worried about Aspen. She was worried about Huldra and Og.

The stage was still open to the field, and the curtains—while still hanging—were frayed and a bit scorched. She forced her stiff legs to clamber up onto the stage and checked the twins' room first, where Aspen stayed. There was no one in there except the strange, animated rug.

Instead of showing its teeth, the rug moaned piteously, obviously frightened by the thunderous noises that had only so recently ceased. The dog boy at the castle had once told her how he hated thunder because all his hounds would try to hide underneath him.

Tentatively, she put out her hand.

"There, there," she said as one would with a hound or a horse. "There, there." The bowser wrapped itself around her legs. It was soft and somewhat cuddly.

"There, there," she said a third time, keeping her voice low and soothing, not wanting the fey creature to even think about biting.

As if the third time was the charm, the bowser gave a little shudder, a soft sigh, then uncurled itself and lay back down on the floor. She reached over to give it a quick pat and felt it sigh under her touch.

Giving the bowser one last pat, one last *There, there*, Snail went back out onto stage. Crossing it quickly she burst into Odds's office without knocking. It, too, was empty. Once onstage again, she looked out onto the battlefield, trying to make out individuals among the bodies, fearful she would see someone she knew.

There was something over to the right, hard to make out at first in the gloaming. Something large, something lying on the ground, something . . .

She felt her heart skip. Her eyes filled with tears.

"Huldra!" she breathed the name, and ran to the edge of the stage, leapt off.

It was only when she was halfway there that she realized she hadn't seen baby Og in the wagon either.

And this was no place for a baby, *any* baby. Certainly not for a troll child she'd just delivered days earlier.

The thought of her newborn charge out here on a battlefield hurried Snail along, and she quickly came in sight of Huldra's feet, then legs, then body, then—thankfully—her head, which was turned away, looking over the misty mountains.

Huldra lay on her stomach, baby Og strapped to her back, where he snored noisily each time he removed his gigantic thumb from his gigantic mouth.

"Huldra!" Snail called aloud. "Can you get up?" The ground around the troll was a bog, wet and rank. Snail put a hand down into the quagmire, brought it to her nose, sniffed blood not mud.

"Alas," Dagmarra said, stepping around from the other side of the hill that was Huldra's head, "she cannot. The wound is in her heart. She waters the ground with her blood."

Snail suddenly noticed that Dagmarra was weeping silently, great globules of tears tracing down her cheeks into her beard.

"She isn't . . ." Snail hesitated before saying more.

"Not dead," Dagmarra said. "At any rate, not yet. But I doubt even the professor can save her."

Nor, Snail thought miserably, *can we turn her over so I can see if the wound can be staunched.* But, by the size of the blood bog around the troll, Snail knew that such an endeavor would only hurt Huldra, not save her. And Mistress Softhands always said that sometimes the greatest kindness was to let the patient go.

"No!" Snail said, not sure if she was agreeing or disagreeing with Dagmarra. "The rest?" she asked fearfully.

"They were fine last I saw. Your prince . . ." Dagmarra paused and looked thoughtful for a moment. "He fought well."

He's not my *prince,* she thought, but didn't say it. Nothing mattered at this moment but Huldra. And Og.

She prepared her most sensible midwife-trained voice. She could still hear Mistress Softhands saying, "No hysterics in the birthing room. And that is especially true for the midwives! No matter what happens, you maintain calm."

"Why can't the professor save her?" Snail asked.

Dagmarra sniffled. "She took too many arrows to the

belly and heart, and some, I fear, may have been tipped with poison."

Snail shook her head. "I've never heard of the Unseelie *archers* using poison," she said, forgetting that just earlier that had been a worry to her. "It would be considered . . ." She thought hard to find the right phrase. Finally ended with "unsporting."

"War isn't sport," Dagmarra said.

"It is to the Border Lords. Could the Seelie soldiers . . ."

"Never, it's considered unhealthy."

"But . . ." And then Snail remembered the poison on Jack Daw's dagger, the dagger that he'd put in the ogre dungeon master's back, the one she'd used by accident on the carnivorous merman.

"If there's poison, I know who might have had a hand in this," Snail said. "But if Huldra is truly dying, we have to take Og from her in case she turns over on him." She doubted Huldra had any such strength left, though there were plenty of stories of trolls doing amazing feats when dying.

"I doubt she has the power left to turn, poor mite," Dagmarra said, stating Snail's thoughts aloud, just as the troll started to shudder.

Huldra groaned and said in a thunderous sigh, "Remember . . . promise me . . ."

Dagmarra hastened back to her head and Snail could hear Dagmarra saying, "I'll honor what I promised, my dear friend. Dinna fash, dinna fash yerself. He will be told, he will give you all honor, he will be *my* boy as well as yours."

There was another loud sigh, like a great wind puzzling through a forest. And with a final shudder, Huldra was still.

Snail untied Og from his mother's back, wrapping him securely in the plaid diaper. She knew what Dagmarra must have promised. But wondered how a dwarf could possibly raise a baby troll.

She was rocking Og in her arms and still thinking this when Dagmarra came back around Huldra's mountain of a body, and held out her hands for the baby.

"Are you sure?" Snail said.

"I'm stronger than I look," Dagmarra said. "And a promise to a friend makes me stronger still."

Snail handed Og to her, and Dagmarra didn't even flinch when the heavy child was in her arms. She looked down at the baby, who was still asleep. "Mama Two loves you," she said. "Your uncles will love you, as well."

As if summoned, Dagmarra's two brothers appeared from the darkness, along with an exhausted but apparently unwounded Aspen. He smiled at her, but the smile never reached his haunted eyes. Snail didn't even try to smile back. Behind him loomed a multi-limbed spider, the professor riding in an odd carapace on its back.

"The battle is over," he called down, as the machine kept marching toward the wagon, "but the war has just begun." He pulled on several levers before him and two of the machine's limbs reached out and began folding the stage back into the wagon. "We make for home as soon as . . ." he looked meaningfully at Snail, "*humanly* possible."

I'm not *human*, she thought, but somehow her arguments, her anger, seemed shallow compared to the misery that had been inflicted on all the people she'd tried to save: Fey or human, Seelie or Unseelie, their races had mattered little in the end. What had mattered was blood and bone and shattered hearts.

ASPEN HAS SOME ANSWERS

cAspen was willing to help pack up the wagon, but there was little he could do but get in the way. After the third time he'd been punched in the arm by one of the dwarfs for stepping on their toes, he took Maggie Light's suggestion to go to the twins' room and lie down. There had been other suggestions, most of them by the dwarfs, but they had nothing to do with packing up the wagon and were all anatomically implausible anyway.

He was so exhausted he entered the wagon from the wrong side and ended up having to travel the length of the wagon to get to the twins' room. There were scorch marks on the walls, and much of what had been stowed carefully was strewn about from the violence of the battle. Nothing seemed broken beyond repair until he reached the dwarfs' room and saw the birdcage lying in the middle of the floor, cracked and partially crushed, its tiny door hanging off its hinges. Beside it lay the bird, motionless.

Somehow, after all the death and violence, it was this small cruelty that finally made Aspen's tears well up. He looked closer, hoping that the bird was only sleeping—*On its side?* he thought. *Are you a child?*—but when he got near he saw a great gash across its breast and its innards spilled onto the wagon's wooden floorboards. But instead of blood and organs, the bird's guts were angular and bright, and the lamplight reflected metallically off of them. He reached out a finger to touch the strange items and snatched it back quickly when a burning sensation hit him.

Cold iron!

He popped his burned finger into his mouth to cool it and his saliva helped soothe the ache.

At the same time, he realized that the bird was not a bird at all. It was some made *thing*. A simulacrum animated, he knew not how or for what reason. He peered at it blankly for a moment more, then realized it was all too much for his tired brain to handle and stumbled away.

Alone in the room, Aspen collapsed onto a bed and closed his eyes. His ears rang from thunderous spells, his throat was sore from shouting, his sword arm ached from the butcher's work of battle.

I should feel better than this, he thought. *We won!*

Or at least, he corrected his mind, *we did not lose.*

But visions of the battle sprang into his head unbidden, and he wondered what victory was worth this price:

*. . . fire takes a peasant girl as she steps between him and the
Border Lord ranks just as he flings his spell . . .*

*. . . a sword cuts at his head, so he ducks and responds, stick-
ing his borrowed sword into the stomach of a Seelie foot soldier
who'd swung at him blindly . . .*

*. . . he is caught in the press and pushes an old brownie away
to clear his sword arm, noticing too late that he has pushed her
right onto the pike of a charging bogle . . .*

He'd killed enemies in the short battle, as well. *Lots of
them,* he thought, trying to feel proud of his courage and
failing. Instead, all he could think of was the spilled blood,
the crack of bone. All he remembered were the faces of the
ones he'd killed, all bearing the same look of surprise and
pain as the allies he'd inadvertently slain. The memories
brought him no relief.

He thought about removing his blood-soaked clothes—
or at least his belt—but his hands were shaking so badly he
didn't think he could manage.

So, he simply lay there trembling, all the while listening
to the screech of the stage sliding back under the wagon,
the whinnies of the unicorns as they were buckled into
their traces, the creak and rumble as the wagon finally got
under way.

Eventually, exhaustion and the rocking of the road got
the better of him and he fell into a deep sleep filled with
lightning, flame, and death.

❖ ❖ ❖

HE AWOKE AT what he thought was dawn. But, when the sky kept getting darker and the sun lower, he realized it was actually sunset of the next day.

I have slept the entire day away and no one has tried to wake me. He wondered if that meant they considered him a prisoner—or a friend.

Maybe they thought I was dead. He pinched his left arm with his right hand. *Nope! Still alive. Lucky they didn't bury me.* He tried a grin at his small joke, failed, and worried he might never smile again.

Even knowing he had slept an entire day did not make him feel rested. He wanted nothing more than to pull the covers over his head and go back to sleep. He tried to find a compelling reason to get out of bed, but could not think of a single one. His escape plan with Snail seemed ludicrous now.

His plan to stop the coming war even more so.

I am as useless as a bull at a birthing, he thought, *and if I lie here forever, the world will likely be improved for it.*

He shut his eyes tight and waited for oblivion to take him again.

❖ ❖ ❖

IT WAS FULLY light the next time he woke. Someone had left waybread and a tankard of water by his bed. He felt no hunger—especially when he saw that the bowser had nibbled on the edges of the bread—but he ate it anyway.

I assume after an entire day and night, my body requires sustenance.

He did feel a *little* better after eating. Though not so good that he thought himself a useful member of the world. But good enough to get up and go outside. Legs weak from lying in bed so long, he staggered to his feet and left the room, only to find himself in Maggie Light's quarters.

Much to his disappointment and relief, Maggie was nowhere to be seen. But a puff of orange-red hair sticking out of the blankets on Maggie Light's bed told him that Snail was asleep.

"Sleep on, my friend," he whispered as quietly as a lullaby. She might not consider him as such, but it suddenly occurred to him that she was truly the only one he could count on. The only one who cared that he was alive in the world.

The dwarfs had not been in their room, but he had expected that. Whenever the wagon was in motion, they were invariably in the driver's seat. Perhaps they even took turns sleeping there.

He left that room and found himself in the professor's quarters. He did not want to see Odds, much less talk to him, so he tiptoed through. Opening the door to the outside, he clambered up to see the dwarfs.

As if to mock his bleak mood, it was a fine, sunny day. The cart now rolled over a smooth track that wandered a short distance across a small, open plain before disappearing into the southwestern mountains.

"What mountains are those?" he said to the dwarfs by way of hello.

Dagmarra's eyes twinkled up at him. "They are *skaap*," she said, her voice a rumble.

"Skaap?" It was not a name or a word he knew.

"Not Seelie." Annar growled the translation.

"Nor Unseelie," Thridi added, his voice not quite as rough.

"Nor the shifting borderlands between," Dagmarra said, twinkle all gone.

Perhaps both kingdoms claim them, Aspen thought.

"Have they a name?"

"Bonebreak," said Annar.

"Or Stonebreak," Thridi told him.

Aspen looked at Dagmarra.

She shrugged. "Or Heartbreak. Choose one. They will break one or all if you try to cross them."

He looked at the craggy dark cliffs and snowcapped heights. *The names could be Seelie or Unseelie. Or perhaps neither.*

"Do we go there?"

"Be hard not to," Annar called back.

"We'd go here but we already are," Thridi added.

Dagmarra was strangely silent.

Aspen was about to restate his question when he noticed that they had company.

"What's that?" he said, pointing to something a short ways ahead of them, shimmering in the sun. "Another wagon?"

"An odd question," Annar said.

"Unless you've gone blind," Thridi said.

"Or it's an ogre in a *very* clever disguise," they said together.

Dagmarra was still silent.

"Yes, well, it's a wagon then," Aspen said, feeling as stupid as he always did when he tried to talk to the dwarfs. But he gave it one more try. "And there are two others, as well. But what are they all doing here?" He held up a hand. "No wait! I know. They're traveling. Getting pulled by horses. Fulfilling their purpose, you might say."

Annar grinned up at Aspen, then poked Thridi. "I'm beginning to like him."

"He *gets* us," Thridi said, grinning as broadly as his brother.

Dagmarra spat spectacularly over the side of the wagon. The spit arced up, turned, and headed downward, its tail glistening in the sunlight like the trail of a flying snail, silver all the way to the ground.

Aspen saw now that there were people walking between the wagons as well. And a few people—a very few—were mounted on bony horses or mules.

He gave careful thought to his next question. "Why are

we and all these others traveling to what seems to be—" He pointed toward the mountains ahead of them. "What seems to be awfully inhospitable territory?"

Annar looked at Thridi, who shrugged. They both looked at their sister, who once more spat over the side of the wagon. Then she shrugged as well.

"Odds is collecting," she said.

"Collecting what?"

"Skarm drema."

The dwarfs all folded their arms and leaned back, and Aspen knew he would not get another word out of them on the subject. He watched the mountains for a while, which seemed to be approaching the wagons rather than the other way around. It was mesmerizing for a few minutes. But soon enough he grew restless and went back to wake up Snail.

❖ ❖ ❖

SNAIL WAS SITTING up in bed, yawning. Aspen smiled at her hair, which looked as if it was trying to escape her scalp. For the first time in days he felt the slightest bit happy.

That feeling lasted just as long as it took Snail to open her mouth.

"What do you know about changelings?" she asked without preamble.

Aspen cocked his head. "Same as you do, I imagine. Though not as *personally*, I suppose."

"What?" Snail screamed at him. "You *knew*?"

He gaped at her. "You did not? How could you *not*? I mean . . ."

"You think I was given a tutor and history lessons like some toff?"

"Well, no but . . ."

"You think the Unseelie spend a lot of time *educating* their servants and underthings?"

"Um . . ."

"Did you think Mistress Softhands would ever tell me that I was *stolen* from my real folks and put right to work?"

He had no answer.

"*That's* how I didn't know."

Aspen held up his hands in an instinctual attempt to stem the flood of angry words. It seemed to work, because when Snail spoke again it was in a lower tone.

"So, tell me," she said again, "what do you know about changelings?"

Her voice might have been lower, but he didn't think she was any calmer.

She asked again, as if issuing a challenge to a duel. "What do *you* know about changelings?"

"What is it you want to know?" he asked.

She shrugged.

He knew very little, but what he did know, he told her, straight out and with nothing held back, friend to . . . well, whatever.

SNAIL MEETS HER CLAN

*A*s Aspen began to speak about changelings, his face turned serious, as if weighing each word and finding it wanting.

"What is it you want to know?" he asked.

Snail was caught short by the question. *What do I want?* The only answer she could come up with was that she wanted to be back to what she was before. *A midwife's apprentice with few friends, but a life ahead of me that I studied for and enjoyed. And tipsy cake. And eating leftovers in the kitchen. And . . .*

Even she had to admit it was a pretty thin list. And as for enjoying her life, well looking back, it had certainly been better than the dungeon, the threat of the dungeon master, the escape across a river of carnivorous mermen, being tied up by a hungry troll, the race ahead of two armies, and the bloody aftermath of a battle.

It looked enjoyable in hindsight, and the truth was that she couldn't go back. This was now, not then. Two armies still searched for her. There was no one trying to keep her safe except an odd professor, an odder singer, three dwarfs, and a useless prince.

So I'd better learn more about this changeling thing. She leaned in toward Aspen and gave him her full concentration.

"Changelings," he was saying, "are human children stolen from their parents and brought into the faery world. And a simulacrum—a piece of wood made to look and act like a child, only badly—is left behind in the cradle or crib in the child's place."

"I know *that* much," Snail said impatiently. "But who stole *me* and how did I end up with Mistress Softhands?"

"Jaunty—my tutor—said that humans are simply better at some things than either the Seelie or Unseelie folk but rubbish at magic. They are better at mathematics and as good as mountain dwarfs at the making of . . ."

"Of . . . ?

"Things."

"Things?"

"Making gates and weaving cloth and brewing good ale and . . ."

"Midwifery?" She could feel herself get icy cold, as if a Frost Giant had laid a hand on her heart. Not that she believed in Frost Giants. They were just bogies to frighten small children into behaving. She used to think the same of changelings.

He nodded. "All kinds of doctoring. For the sorts of illnesses that can't be cured with spells. I do not know about midwives. Were your midwife tutors changelings?"

"They could do spells."

"Then probably not." He shook his head, but his face didn't change, so she had no way of knowing if he was lying to her.

Snail couldn't tell if she was shaking because the wagon was moving or because she was all a-tremble, finally deciding it was both. "Tell me more. Tell me how *I* came here."

"I cannot say for certain." His voice got lower as if he was ashamed of something. "I would have been only a child myself and living at the Seelie Court then."

"Well . . ." She could feel her face now turning hot, sure that her cheeks were suddenly ablaze. That happened with redheads. And, now that she thought of it, didn't seem to happen to anyone truly fey. They only got whiter or pink, or looked confused, or downright angry. They didn't carry a fire on their cheeks.

"Well, what?" He looked truly puzzled.

"Well, what did your *tutor* have to say about that?"

He looked down at his feet, and the wagon made a sudden lurch at the same time. She saw something shift in his face, as if he had decided to lie to her and then decided it would not be a noble thing to do.

"Jaunty," she prompted. "Your Unseelie tutor?"

He looked up, and his eyes almost held tears. "He said that because the Seelie folk look more like humans than most Unseelie, we are the ones who go into the human world and steal the children. To order. Only he didn't say *steal*. As I recall, he said *collect*. The Seelie folk *collect* the human children and bring them to a central tower, and then when there are enough to make it worth their while, the Seelie collectors take the changelings into the Shifting Lands and sell them to . . ."

Snail interrupted. "Sold? I was *sold*?"

He nodded miserably.

"How do you know. . . ?" And then she stopped herself. Aspen, as the Hostage Prince, probably made much the same journey. She could ask him, she supposed. It might hurt him to remember.

And then she shook her head. *This isn't about him. It's about me.* Only she had no memory of being taken, sold, exchanged. The hurt, whatever it had been then, was suddenly here. Now. And it wasn't a hurt at all but a blazing anger.

"You know," he said suddenly, "it was actually better that way than the Unseelie going into the human world. I mean, some of them get hungry and eat . . ."

She turned away, furious with him. He just didn't think that anyone beneath his rank might have feelings. That they might have had parents who loved them, mourned them.

Over her shoulder she said, "Better that *collecting* didn't happen at all. Just leave me alone, your royal high mucky-muck. Go away. I just don't want to talk to you anymore."

She lay back down on the bed and pulled the covers over her head, counting slowly to a hundred.

Very slowly.

When she was done, she peeked out and saw that she was alone in the room.

"Good," she said. Though she knew it wasn't. Not really.

❖ ❖ ❖

THERE WAS A dress laid out on the bed. Snail doubted Aspen had left it there.

Maggie Light probably had. She was glad to change because her own clothes were crusted with the blood of all the wounds she'd treated.

She pumped water from the small cistern and washed her hands and face and the parts of her arms that were blood-soaked as well. She'd never been as dirty as this that she could remember. Midwives simply weren't allowed to get dirty. And after every birth, they got to soak for a long time in a tub of heated water. Even in the dungeon she hadn't been this filthy. Nor helping Huldra birth baby Og. Nor climbing the chimney while trying to escape from the Seelie castle. Nor traipsing through the fields and the bog. Nor . . .

She dried herself with a cloth hanging on a hook by the cistern and put on the dress. It was made of a soft, dark blue cotton that matched one of her eyes, with green threads shooting through the sleeves that matched the other eye.

There was an apron, too, not striped like her apprentice apron, but a lighter shade of the blue and somewhat stiffer. Plus a pair of blue hose.

Nothing could be done about her shoes.

She took the brush that had been set out on a small table next to the cistern and attacked her hair until she beat it into submission. At last she was ready to go outside.

❖ ❖ ❖

WHAT GREETED HER was a surprise. During her long sleep, the wagon must have come an enormous distance. They were now in a kind of large bowl set between high mountains.

In the bowl, buzzing like honey ants in a broken mound, were hundreds—maybe even thousands—of folk who, she had to assume, were changelings just like her.

She could see some of them were bandaged, and as she walked amongst them, they waved and shouted out their thanks. But others seemed untouched by any battles and hardly noticed her passage.

Cook-fires glowed all around. And families—or what passed for families, for she realized that many of the groups consisted of young people just her age—were busy cooking in great metal pots, not the usual pottery pans that the fey used for their meals.

The smells were enticing. She thought there might be onions and wild garlic and herbs for seasoning. But what meat in the pot she couldn't begin to guess. Venison or boar or rabbit or squirrel or . . .

She checked that the unicorns were still tethered close to Odds's wagon and was relieved to see them there, comfortably grazing on the grass.

Too new at being a changeling—a human she supposed she should call herself—she found she was shy about speaking to any of the families. Just nodded and smiled.

She started to turn back to Odds's wagon when a girl a bit younger than she came up, equally shyly, and held out her hand.

"Will you eat with us, physician?" she asked.

Snail thought for a moment that the girl was talking to someone else, someone behind her. But when the girl took her hand, Snail had to admit the invitation was for her.

She resisted saying that she was no physician, only a midwife's apprentice. She'd already brought one baby—one very big baby—into the world. And she had bandaged many a battle wound, saving limbs and saving lives as best she could. She supposed she was, in fact, some kind of physician/midwife now. Mistress Softhands often said, "A midwife is born in the birthing room as surely as the baby."

Meaning, she now realized, *that until you have been through the worst of it on your own, you cannot really claim the title.* And both the troll baby's birth and the battle doctoring she'd done on her own. Learning as she went, and making up the rest.

Bowing her head quickly, she said, "I would be honored. Call me Sofie." It was the first thing that came into her mind.

The girl head-bobbed back.

Sofie. That was something she was never called, though it was her name. Mistress Softhands had used it once or twice. But it was as if Snail—the Snail who was awkward and uncomfortable and accident-prone—had died in the battle, the Seelie War, and Sofie had been reforged in its fire.

Sofie. It was an odd name. Meaningless. Maybe that's why no one in the Unseelie Court ever called her that—just Snail and Useless and You There. And, once, *Duck.* Though that was less a name than a call for her to get out of the way of a flying object. She hadn't ducked fast enough and they all thought that was hilariously funny, so for a while it had become her name amongst the other apprentices.

Duck.

Well, she thought, *I'll have to give the name Sofie meaning. It will be my own invention. It will simply mean what I want it to mean.*

And so thinking, she went over to meet and eat with some of the members of her clan.

ASPEN CHANGES PLANS . . . AGAIN

They hate me, Aspen thought, looking out the wagon's peephole at the hordes of humans in the camp. He told himself this not with sadness, but with a careful thoughtfulness, and not for the first time. He supposed that all the human changelings he'd ever met had probably hated him but had been much better at hiding it. Or he had never cared to notice. But here amongst their own, in numbers Aspen had not known existed, they had no reason to hide their feelings. And because of Snail, he now cared.

Whenever he left the wagon, the humans sneered at him, turning their backs and talking in pointed whispers. Young men gathered in groups and stared angrily at him, and he knew it was only the stories the battle survivors told of the fire he commanded that kept them from setting upon him. Fear kept them away, kept him safe.

But how long will that last? And if they do have at me, do I dare to wield the flame again?

He was no longer worrying about the two courts' wizards finding him. They would be busy with the war that had so obviously started. He guessed that if the wizards had still been searching for him, they would have appeared in the days after the battle, arriving in puffs of smoke, or flying in on giant bats' wings, or riding fell creatures summoned from the void.

And what would I do if they come now? Aspen wondered. He saw what happened when he drew sword or wielded flame. He could not get the cries out of his head.

A peasant girl screaming . . . a soldier coughing blood . . . a bogle's surprised face when an old brownie is pushed onto his pike by her ally.

He did not know if he could ever go through that horror again.

Aspen watched through the peephole until Maggie Light brought him a bowl of something spicy to eat. He thanked her and choked it down, though it was obviously made for a more *earthy* palate than his own. Would he ever eat hummingbird breast again, crispy rose petals, sugared violets? Would he ever have another cup of honey mead?

He tried one more time to leave the wagon and speak to the humans, tell them that he wasn't there to hurt them or rule them, he just wanted to find his friend—his human friend—and find out if she would still speak to him.

But the men who followed him this time had cudgels and cold iron knives, and he hurried back to the wagon before they were able to get too close. No matter how they dealt with him in camp, none had yet dared to follow him into the wagon. He realized suddenly that if Odds removed his protection, he would not make it through another night. He wondered how long the professor's good will would last.

Or is it good will? he thought morosely. The man talked in riddles. Perhaps he thought in them as well.

Climbing up the back end of the wagon, Aspen thought, *Odds may not even know what use he has for me yet. Perhaps he sees me as a valuable piece in whatever game he is playing.*

Suddenly he had a revelation. *Is that not what I have always been: a valuable game piece—for my father, for King Obs, for Jack Daw?*

It felt as if an icy hand was palm down on his back, and he wondered if cold iron was about to sever his neck.

Perhaps, he thought, *that might be the best way out. At least dead I could no longer be used by anyone.*

But his body had its own agenda—and that was to keep itself alive. Without willing it, he had already ducked through the door.

He felt the bowser before he saw it, for it scrunched up and wrapped itself around his knees.

"What if the professor decides I'm not that valuable after all?" He said that aloud, which caused the bowser to squeeze his knees even more, as if it was afraid to lose him.

It was then he thought that he really had to leave. Even if he never spoke to Snail again, it was the right thing to do.

For her sake.

For his own.

❖ ❖ ❖

ASPEN SPENT THE next day trying to have a quiet word with Snail, but she never approached the wagon. He was sure she saw him waving to her—from the back door, from the dwarfs' driving porch, from the roof—but she never acknowledged him. Never so much as blinked before turning and walking away, usually surrounded by at least a half-dozen well-wishers.

He finally figured out that she was sleeping at the campfires with the other humans, pointedly staying away from the wagon. In his good moments, he thought she might be avoiding Odds. But in his bad moments, he knew she was avoiding him.

That night, he made the actual decision to leave.

It is better that way. She has found her people and should stay with them. At that moment, Aspen realized that he no longer knew who his people were.

I'm not a toff anymore, though all here would call me so. And I cannot be one of those here, for I do not know how. He made a face and told himself the bitter truth. *We do not have the same blood. We do not have the same gifts. We do not . . .*

Then told himself the *real* truth. *They would not have me anyway.*

So, if he was leaving, he would need supplies for his jour-

ney. He would need a new plan. The old one had been useless anyway. He hoped he would need no help, because he
knew he would not get any.

❖ ❖ ❖

FAR INTO THE night, he made his preparations. With a
waterskin and the watcher's green-and-black cloak he found
stuffed under Maggie Light's bed, a traveling pack, three
days' worth of waybread stolen carefully from the wagon's
stores plus the bow and quiver of arrows he had used
to hunt the deer for the troll, he waited for the camp to
settle down. There would still be sentries posted, but they
would be watching for enemies *approaching* the camp, not
leaving it.

He would leave through the back of the wagon, which
faced the nearby dense woods. Once into the woods, he
could slip on the cloak and fade into the wilderness.

And then where?

He stopped that line of thought immediately. He only
knew he had to leave. Everything else he would figure out
later.

Or not figure out.

Shrugging, he thought, *It is not as if anyone will mourn
me if I wander into the wilds and die.*

He had already forgotten his earlier wish to die, and
quashed those thoughts. *I need to concentrate on the one
obstacle left: the dwarfs.*

He wasn't sure if they had any orders regarding him. *Will they try to follow me? Stop me from leaving? Alert Odds?* He had no idea.

"Only one way to find out," he muttered, and opened the door of the wagon.

He was two steps out when he heard Dagmarra's voice calling to him. "Where away, popinjay?"

He turned slowly and looked up. Only Dagmarra sat on the driver's perch. Perhaps her brothers were off with the humans. They seemed to have no trouble interacting with them.

"What?" He sounded stupid, even to himself.

Dagmarra pulled a pipe from a pouch in her belt and began searching for a flint and tinder. "I *said*, where away? You seem rather well equipped for an evening stroll."

Having no other reply ready, he answered with the simple truth. "I do not know."

"Hrmmm," Dagmarra said. She'd found flint and tinder and looked at them wistfully for a moment before *not* lighting her pipe. "I'll walk with ye. I don't like yer chances alone with the skarm drema. And your girl will sever my head if I let anything happen to you."

Aspen felt a strange glow at the thought that Snail would care that much. But he quashed that thought, too. Concentrate, he told himself.

He thought about his chances of walking about the encampment without a guard like Dagmarra. They were better if she was along. But . . . if she realized he was abandoning the camp without the professor's permission . . .

However, he thought, *it is odd that she would act as my friend of a sudden, as if caring for a child has made her motherly toward me, as well.* It was a puzzle, and he set his mind to figuring it out.

And suddenly he knew what to do.

"I would appreciate your company," he said, bowing politely. "But are you sure Og should be wandering about on his own?"

"What?" Dagmarra sputtered. "He doesn't walk yet!"

"But I just saw him through the peephole, crawling off toward the fires. You know how babies are fascinated by fires." He worried that the last confabulation might be a bit too much. He had no idea if babies were drawn to flames. But then, perhaps Dagmarra did not either.

Evidently, she did not doubt him for an instant, for pipe, flint, and tinder rattled onto the wagon boards as she leapt off the far side.

Aspen heard her thump to the ground moments later and hoped she had not injured herself; it was a far longer fall for her than it would have been for him.

But the sound of her footsteps hurrying away from the wagon assured him that while she was clearly unhurt, he had best be long away before she discovered Og still sleeping in the wagon where she'd left him. In fact, the baby's only danger came from the large puddle of drool he was almost certainly leaving on the pillow.

Aspen pulled the cloak out of his pack and wrapped it around his shoulders, trying not to shudder at the thought of how its original owner had died. He could feel the shadows calling to the magic in the cloak and he didn't resist, following their pull quickly and quietly into the dark, concealing forest.

As he walked through the night, Aspen felt safe for the first time in days. Even though he was no night-sighted Unseelie, he was still an elf and the Seelie forests were his ancestral home. The dark was not something to fear but was as concealing as the cloak. He found easy footing and a trail that beckoned him forward.

By the time the sun was rising, he had the feel of the ground underfoot, recognized the call of the birds, and had charted the course of the stars overhead. Only when he felt far enough away from the camp did he rest. By then, he was exhausted.

I will take my chances, he thought. And wrapping the cloak completely around him, he crawled into the underbrush, falling quickly asleep.

The sun was high overhead when he woke. He broke off a piece of waybread and chewed it while walking again. But oddly the sun did not seem to be moving.

Magic, he thought, and after an hour of walking through

the woods, he realized he had no idea in which direction he was going in.

He gave a short, sharp hough through his nose. *And I do not care. What does it matter?*

He thought about his meager supplies. *I shall wander till my food runs out and then I shall hunt.* It was as good a plan as any other.

❖ ❖ ❖

AFTER HE HAD walked for another hour, the sun had begun to move again. Whatever wizards' battle had happened was either won or lost, done or undone. But at least now he realized he was heading north.

The forest was still thick, but he thought it might be thinning as the terrain rose, and he began to wonder what he would see when he reached the top of the long hill he'd begun to climb.

He looked ahead but could not see what lay beyond the trees. *I will know soon enough.*

A half hour later, the trees indeed thinned out, and when he reached the top of the hill he had been climbing—he was secretly relieved it wasn't a mountain—he looked out onto a wide plain.

A few miles to his right, he could see the track they had followed from Bogborough to the humans' camp. There was still smoke on the horizon there. Aspen wondered if the town still burned.

To his left, the mountains faded into the plains, and he could see the thin green line of the Welcome Hedge, though it, too, was shrouded in smoke, as if parts of it burned as well.

But it was the plain that riveted his attention, for down below were two huge armies separated still by many miles but moving ponderously toward one another.

The Unseelie army had finally brought his father to battle.

Now he understood why the sun had stood so long in the middle of the sky. The wizards hadn't been warring. They were too evenly matched for that. They had been testing the other army's strength, its generals' commitment to the fight, the battle readiness of the men.

Why fight here? he wondered. *Here, so far away from either kingdom's seat of power. What brings them to this empty place to decide the outcome of the Seelie war?*

He tried to think of the advantages, the plots, the machinations that brought them to this spot, but in his heart, he knew the answer.

Me.

He had not escaped the notice of wizards and spies. When he cast the flames in Bogborough, the wizards *had* seen him. And when he'd drawn his weapon, spies *had* noticed him. Perhaps the cloaked man had even sent a message by pigeon or by hawk.

Both courts, both armies, both councils of wizards had come for him. But instead of finding him, they had found one another.

And where wizards and spies went, the armies followed.

Now, between the two large armies, smaller groups clashed, looking like colonies of ants from this distance.

"Skirmishers." He remembered Jaunty naming them in one of his history lessons. Scouts and rangers who check the ground and test the strength of the enemy lines before a battle.

"Is their work really that vital?" he had asked.

"They fight just to blood the foe," the old tutor had said, somewhat wearily, "so no one has to work to reach battle fury on the morrow. Use your imagination, my prince. I know you have it in abundance."

But do I? he wondered, and stared at the scene below, trying to match what he was seeing with the pictures drawn on Jaunty's battle scrolls.

All of a sudden, Aspen understood how long it would take for the two larger bodies of fighters, most of them foot soldiers, to reach the enemy lines. The skirmishers were more mobile, swifter. They could turn and return at will. Jaunty had been absolutely right. All the skirmishers needed to do was to bloody one or two of the outliers in the army to unsettle them, make them fear what was to come.

They will fight tomorrow, he thought, *but they will remember their bloodied companions. And they will forget their order and be careless with their own lives.*

Once again, he remembered his pledge to stop this war. A prince's pledge. Promises made in haste, Jaunty had warned him once, are most often repented in sorrow. He thought about that.

Just a day ago he had dismissed his pledge as impossible, undoable, even foolish. But Fate or Mab's justice or sheer stupidity had brought him to this place and time. Somehow there was a reason. There was no such thing as coincidence on this scale.

And what was that reason?

In a lightning moment, he knew what it was: He had to fulfill his pledge, foolish or otherwise, and there was just one night left to do it.

29

SNAIL HEARS ODDS'S BIG SPEECH

"*He*'s gone?" Snail asked. "What do you *mean,* gone?"
She'd noticed Aspen skulking for a while on the outskirts of
the campsites, then figured he'd realized no one wanted to
invite him to sit for a meal or a natter, so he'd most probably
settled into the wagon, in his toffy-nosed, standoffish way.

But two days later, when the worst of her anger was behind
her, and she'd decided to try and talk to him in a reason-
able fashion, she couldn't find him. She'd already circled the
encampment five times and checked into the wagon at least
that often, asking each guard and lookout. None had seen
him, though one had grunted, "Good riddance to that elf
rubbish."

That's when she'd begun to worry. He was, after all,
her first real and truest friend, no matter what arguments
they'd had. They'd saved each other from dungeons and
torture and carnivorous mermen, from hungry trolls, two
armies, and . . .

And yet when he'd told her the unvarnished truth about where she came from, she'd tried to skewer him for the messenger he was, instead of railing at the message.

It was Dagmarra who informed her that he was, in fact, gone.

"Tricked me, by Oberon's beard," the dwarf said. "Gone these two days." She was burping little Og across her knees in the dwarfs' bedroom. He was almost as big as Dagmarra now, and must—Snail thought—be quite a burden to carry. But Dagmarra didn't mind. In fact, she seemed besotted with him.

Little Og! He'll never *be little*, Snail reminded herself. *He's a troll.*

Then she asked, "But where did Aspen go?" She was horrified that she couldn't keep the whine out of her voice.

Now Dagmarra shouldered Og to finish the burping job. The sound he made when the burp was finally dislodged was loud enough to wake anyone in the wagon, and that included the bowser, who growled loudly.

"I don't know, but I can guess." Dagmarra spoke in what—for her—was a growl as well, though it was much quieter than Og's burp.

"Where . . . ?"

"Back to the Unseelie Court where he belongs. As a hostage."

"He can't do that, they'll . . ." Snail's hand went over her mouth without her willing it.

"Kill him? As well they should," said Dagmarra. "No one tricks me and lives!"

"He would *never* go back to that awful place," Snail said with an absolute conviction she realized she didn't have.

Dagmarra put the baby onto her bed. He was asleep again, with a little bead of goat's milk falling from his lower lip instead of drool.

Turning to Snail, Dagmarra shook her head. "He's a prince. They do all kinds of stupid things and call it noble."

What the dwarf had just said seemed to fizz in Snail's head, like fresh water drunk straight out of a waterfall. "That's it!" Snail declared. "That's it. He's gone off to do the most foolish, noble thing he can think of."

"And what's that, if not to give himself over to the ghastly Unseelie crew?"

"No, no—he's gone off to stop the entire war."

Dagmarra snorted through her nose, which made baby Og open his eyes and give a loud cry, before falling immediately back to sleep again. "One prince . . . one *boy*! How can he stop an entire war?"

"I don't know," Snail said. "But I hope he succeeds."

Dagmarra looked at Snail strangely, then said, "You might feel different after the professor's announcement tonight."

Snail knew the camp had been abuzz with guesses, though no one actually seemed to have a clue as to what Odds was going to say. But as one woman with long yellow braids piled like a crown atop her head had said, "This is the reason we've been called here!" On that point, all the people near her had agreed.

Except for Snail. "Why would anything Odds says change how I feel?" But saying that aloud had made her feel stupid. Hadn't the last thing Odds had told her—about her being a stolen human child—changed her forever?

Now Dagmarra just shook her head. "I know yer smart, girl. I can tell, with the doctoring and all. And solving those bewitched puzzles the old man throws about. And I know yer brave, too. I've seen you in the battles. But don't try to go against the professor. He thinks on a level far above the likes of us."

"What do you mean?"

"I mean I've known him my whole life. He pulled my brothers and me out of war and poverty when we were just babes. He saved us and raised us, and I'd die for him. My brothers, too." She looked down at her pipe, then back at Snail. "But that doesna mean he'd do the same for us."

"That doesn't seem fair."

Dagmarra chuckled. "Fair's a human thing. Not a fey notion. You're skarm drema for sure." Still chuckling, she left the room.

Snail gazed after her. *I thought Odds was human, too. So why isn't he fair?* And then she wondered if she was thinking of fairness in the wrong way, through the eyes of friendship, not the eyes of the real world.

❖ ❖ ❖

SNAIL WAITED THE long day, her thoughts flitting like spring birds. She worried about Aspen. He was truly clueless when it came to dealing with people, and she feared he'd gone off and gotten himself into trouble that even his princely powers couldn't get him out of.

I should never have ignored him, she thought. *I should have left* with *him. I've been selfish and . . .* Then just as quickly, she excused herself: *He didn't tell me he was leaving!*

Now her worry turned to anger and she stomped around the wagon muttering to herself until Dagmarra threatened to tie her to a chair if she woke the baby.

So she went outside and wandered the camp for a while, but her newfound friends could sense her mood, somewhere between anger and despair, and kept their distance.

By the time evening fell, Snail was in a truly foul temper, and hungry as well.

Heading back to the wagon, she saw that it once again had been transformed into a stage, and she hadn't even noticed that happening.

"How could I not?" she asked herself. There must have been the groaning of the wagon sides as the stage went up. The clabber of the metal spider. The jabber of the humans watching.

But she'd been on the far side of the camp, deep in her own thoughts, mired in guilt. Trying to figure out Aspen's plans, trying to think what she could possibly say once she'd caught up with him.

Because she *had* to find him. Had to tell him that they were friends no matter what.

She looked again at the stage.

This time there were no actors up there, no Aspen in his princess dress or Dagmarra in her princely outfit, or the dragon with its drooping wings. This time only Professor Odds stood at the front. He wore a scholar's robe, and it made him look somehow regal. When he held out his arms for silence, the crowd complied, and Snail felt herself go quiet as well.

"Well met, good people," Odds said. He spoke normally, but his voice filled the clearing, and the people around Snail muttered back, "Well met."

Snail alone was silent, arms crossed over her chest.

"We are called mud-folk, changelings, lowest of the low," Odds said, then paused a beat. "They say we are peasants, servants, slaves, born that way and deserving of nothing else." He paused another beat.

The crowd held its collective breath.

"We are not."

For once he's not speaking in riddles, she thought, and wondered if he'd written this speech out beforehand or was speaking from the heart.

That presumes, she thought, *that he has a heart!*

She could see the people in the audience nodding with the rhythm of his words. They were definitely understanding what he was telling them. And something more. It was as if he was casting a spell over them, but he'd told her he'd no skill with magic.

Maybe he lied.

"We call ourselves human even if we have only tasted—however briefly—the untainted air of our homeland." He lifted his head as if he could smell the human world on the wind. "But we are more than that." He looked back at the crowd. "We are skarm drema."

All around her Snail heard the humans mumble the name, skarm drema. The hairs on her arm tingled. There were unbidden tears in her eyes.

It has to be magic, she thought, furiously wiping the tears away.

As if unaware of how his words were working, Odds kept speaking. "That's what the dwarfs call us. 'Free ones.' For each of us has drawn at least one free breath in our life-time." He looked around and drew in a huge breath.

The crowd did the same.

Even Snail found herself taking a big breath, filling her lungs with the air of freedom. As soon as she realized what she was doing—what Odds was doing *to* her—she exhaled sharply.

"But that," Odds said, "is not enough. Not enough for me!" His fists were clenched now, and he shouted the next line at the audience. "Is it enough for you?"

"No!" the crowd shouted back, and Snail shouted with them, caught up again in the injustice of it all.

Dragged from my home, she thought bitterly, *taken to another land and enslaved . . .* She stopped, afraid that Odds's spell had really caught her now. She shook her head as if to dislodge any magic there, but she knew, deep down, that it was not magic. Aspen had essentially told her the same thing. She was hearing true words, spoken well.

Is that the power humans *have?*

Odds raised his hands and the crowd quieted once more. "We are Free Ones in mind. Tonight we shall become Free Ones in body as well."

The woman with the yellow braids shouted, "How?" at the stage, and others cried out, "It's impossible!"

Odds frowned at the naysayers before smiling benevolently down at the rest of the crowd. "Of *course* it's impossible. They have armies and magic and power beyond our imagining. If we try to attack the Seelie Court, their wizards can curse us and their warriors will pierce us with arrows. If we attack the Unseelie Court, the Border Lords can crush us, their bogies can eat us, and King Obs will decorate his walls with whatever is left over." He hung his head dramatically and waited for the audience to settle.

It took a while, but soon the crowd began hushing and shushing itself.

That's when Odds looked up again, a playful grin dancing across his features. "That's why we're going to attack both courts together."

Now the shouts turned to, "You're mad!" but Snail didn't

join in. Whatever the professor's plan was, she didn't think it would actually involve a heroic but doomed assault on both foes.

Odds let the dissension in the crowd grow till Snail was sure he'd lost them.

"You say I'm mad," he said softly, almost too softly to be heard over the hubbub of the unsettled crowd.

Snail strained to hear. She wasn't alone. As the crowd quieted almost immediately, she suddenly realized Odds's speaking so softly was a trick. In fact, everything about him was tricksy. He wasn't a wizard, but he knew human magic—sleight of hand, evasions, half-truths.

And it was working.

Instead of trying to shout the crowd down—which they might have fought against—he's making them a party to the task. She thought about everything that had happened since she and Aspen had joined Odds's troupe and wondered how often he'd used this skill on them.

The crowd was listening intently now, visibly moving closer to the stage, jostling to get closer to the man, as if they suddenly loved and worshipped him. Snail was pulled along on the tidal wave of their humanity.

Odds went on. "Of course I'm mad. But is it madder than living in slavery? Is it madder than lying down to those who have wronged you, offering your throat to the fangs of the fey like servile dogs?"

Slowly, but surely his voice grew louder. "Is it madder

than failing to see what is plainly before you: a chance to finally be free?" He shouted the last words but quickly held up his hand before the crowd could shout with him.

"Here is what you don't see." He pointed toward the horizon. "Even now, the great armies of the two courts prepare to meet on the field of battle. They are well matched. Tomorrow, perhaps the day after that, they will fight. Weapons will clash, blood will flow, great energies will be expended. When the battle is over, the victors—whoever they are—will lie exhausted on the field, sure in the knowledge that they have finally secured the safety of their kingdom."

Now there was a complete hush throughout the crowd. Snail felt that hush as a living thing, the breath of a mob before it explodes.

"They will not have done any such thing."

Bonfires flared to life on both sides of the stage, and the light of the new flames illuminated a trio of giant metal spiders that had marched up behind the wagon in the darkness.

Snail saw small figures riding in each carapace. After a moment, she realized they were the dwarfs, though their faces were disguised by hoods.

Suddenly, there was a thundering of hooves, and a large cart drawn by two horses and driven by two more dwarfs forced the onlookers into two separate columns. The horses galloped into the middle of the crowd, but with such skill, no one was hurt.

Snail recognized Annar as he leapt from the driver's seat into the back of the cart, flipping three times like an acrobat. She looked again at the dwarfs riding on the spiders and realized that they were nothing more than made things, not real at all but puppets of sticks and cloth.

There was a tremendous noise, and she turned to see that Annar had already kicked the back of the cart open, and a huge store of metal objects spilled out onto the grass. Swords, pikes, armor, shields—enough gear to outfit a small army.

Which, Snail thought as she looked around the crowded camp, *is what Odds has created.*

As if echoing her thoughts, Odds said, "There is a third army. An army of Free Ones. You, my brothers and sisters, my friends! And once the two fey armies have fought, when their warriors are exhausted and their magicks spent, when their dead litter the field in the thousands . . ." His grin was wide and toothy now, his teeth reflecting red in the fire's light. "Then the army nobody has suspected exists shall fall upon them, and harvest them like autumn wheat. We shall slaughter every last one of them and they will taste our thousand-year vengeance!"

The crowd roared at this and surged forward, grabbing up arms and armor. Snail was about to join them when Odds spoke again.

"But we will not stop there! With the fey armies defeated, even the weak humans, the ones who were born into Faerie, the halflings, the quarterlings, will join us. We will have numbers, then, and we will invade the weakened kingdoms. We will kill the strong, enslave the weak. Their women and children will serve us. And there will never be war or slavery again!"

The crowd was roaring along with Odds now, but something had suddenly made Snail's stomach queasy. She needed to think quietly, to figure out what was wrong.

But there was no quiet here, no time for thinking. Only time for action, response.

Someone pressed a sword into her hand and she looked up to see the girl who'd first called her "physician" and welcomed her into camp. The girl's eyes were wide and gleaming, and Snail thought that if Odds asked her right now to go stab a family member, the girl would do it and thank him for the order.

That's when Snail remembered something Mistress Softhands had told her a long time ago: "Pain begets pain. Every pain you cause outside the birthing chamber will eventually find its way *into* the birthing chamber. You are a healer now, so cause as little pain as possible."

Pain begets pain, she thought.

"Excuse me!" she shouted. "I have to ask something." It was hard to be heard over the excited crowd. But Snail knew that Odds had heard because he turned toward her, frowning. Then he looked away.

"Hey!" Snail shouted. "I want to ask something, professor!"

Odds studiously ignored her, but the girl who'd given her the sword shouted, "The physician wants to speak!"

Others joined her. "Physician! Let the physician speak."

Their shouts quickly became a chant that the crowd took up. "Physician! Physician! Physician!"

Snail looked around and saw that many who were shouting for her to be heard had been her patients. There was the farmer whose leg she'd sewn up. There, the girl she'd taken an arrow out of. A broken nose she'd set, a shoulder put back in the socket, a long gash down the side bandaged.

These people, she thought, *might respect Odds, might be ready to follow him into danger and death, but they'd not felt his healing hands on them in their darkest hours.*

The crowd finally stopped its chant and waited for Snail to speak. Even Odds waited, though his face was stormy.

"How will more war and slavery put an end to war and slavery?" she asked.

Odds smiled at that, as if at a small child, but it was not a nice smile.

And I'm not a child, Snail thought.

"It ends for us when they can't force us for their ends," Odds said, off his script and sounding like himself again. "We are not they, and fey are not we, though some are wee in stature, at least. *We* have restraint, *they* only restrain.

We do not steal children!" He paused and pointed at her, drawing her into his argument, making her a part of his counterpoint. "We *heal* them. We only punish the punishers. Enslave only those who enslaved us."

Snail saw many in the crowd were now nodding in agreement. She *almost* agreed herself. But still, there had to be another way. She tried again.

"Why can't we just go home? Why fight a battle we may not win? Or if we do win, will turn us into what we hate: murderers and slavers. We were taken here, as you rightly point out. Surely we are strong enough and free enough to take ourselves home?"

"Oh, my children," Odds said, sounding like the father Snail had never known, "you know so little. Time moves differently in our two worlds. If we were to step through the gate, we would all crumble to dust before we ever set foot in our former home."

There was a sudden and horrible hush in the crowd as they thought about what Odds had just said.

"You don't know that," Snail cried out. As she said it, she saw in his eyes that he didn't. "You *think* that, but you don't know for sure. It's just one of many possibilities, isn't it?"

He opened his mouth to speak, but Snail shouted him down. "And what about the gate? And where is it? Shouldn't we find it and try to go home through it, instead of fighting and killing and dying just to become what we most despise?"

The crowd all turned to Odds for the answer, and Snail saw that this time his face held not a subtle storm but a towering rage. For a moment. Only a moment. Then the peaceful, paternal smile was back.

"Let me explain my Trans-World Gate Theory and why we cannot return. It's a simple thing, really, where F equals the rate of time flow and Y equals the amount of time spent in Faerie. There is a random factor as well, something to do with the amount of magic expended during the moment of entry. It is represented by X and can never be known with any certainty . . ."

He droned on, but Snail was never to know the full theory. For as soon as the crowd had all turned to hear the professor speak, a rag was suddenly shoved over her nose and mouth. It smelled of pine and honey and made her immediately and immensely tired.

The last thing she heard before passing out was Maggie Light's voice in her ear.

"Alas, dear child. I was made to do as I am told."

ASPEN'S BEST-LAID PLANS

*A*spen spent nearly the whole night thinking and plotting and going round in circles to try to discover a way to stop the battle that would surely come with the dawn.

Part of the reason he had hardly slept was that he was cold. Especially his ears.

Fey ears, he thought, *always blue-up first. If I were a drow or a Red Cap or . . .* Even the cloak around his head had done little to keep his ears warm.

Finally, as the sun was just edging over the horizon, he sat hunched over, clutching his knees. Giving up on sleep, he gave thought to the war.

There is nothing I can do.

A single tear rolled down his cheek.

Unmanly, he thought. *Ignoble. Here I am, young and alone and faced with the legendary stubbornness of my father on one side, the evil cunning of Old Jack Daw on the other side. If only I were smart like Professor Odds or old Jaunty.*

He let go of his knees and sat straight up. The sun's rays struck him as hard as that last thought had.

Jaunty! He's a king's counselor. Not a high one, but certainly ranked high enough to travel with the court to the greatest battle Faerie had seen in a thousand years. That is, if he hasn't been executed for teaching me treason.

Aspen stood, stretching out his cramped legs. *I will sneak into camp and find him. Surely if I explain what has happened he will think of something.*

It was not much of a plan, but having any plan at all filled him with a rapturous joy. He chomped two bits of waybread and wrapped himself again in his cloak. Figuring that no one would be watching for him magically while preparing for the coming battle, he cast a few minor spells of concealment.

The horns were already calling the troops to battle and the sound quickened his steps. Before the sun had fully breached the horizon, he was down the hill and sneaking up on the Unseelie camp.

Because he wore the cloak of a spy, he knew he would be fairly invisible in the woods. The small spells would complete his disguise. Still, he dreaded running into sentries. A wrong word, a misstep, and he could be unmasked. He was not well schooled in concealment.

His real hope lay in the fact that most Unseelie creatures were uncomfortable in the daylight, sun-blinded. Except for the Border Lords. But they—always eager for battle, crazy for it—would already be out on the field, making up the front lines.

Briefly, he wondered why King Obs was allowing the fight to take place in the day, and not riding out upon the Seelie forces in the middle of the night.

Possibly so he can force my father to attack with his smaller force.

He shook his head. *More probably so the Seelie folk can watch in complete horror as they are cut down.* Aspen had no doubt who the winner of today's battle was going to be.

He could see the camp banners, now dark and tattered, flying over grey tents. He found the king's tent first, bigger than the rest with a large black banner overhead that featured a red splotch for the blood of Obs's enemies. A crow emblem on a grey flag flew on the tent next door. That would be Old Jack Daw's flag. Aspen shuddered.

Old Jack Daw. Whom he'd once thought was his friend. His *only* friend.

Well, I have no friends now.

Other councilors' flags fluttered over slightly smaller tents, with the emblems of boars and beasts and bloody heads dancing in the light breeze.

Aspen searched for Jaunty's symbol, a quill pen dipped in blood, and finally saw it off on the edges, almost among the common soldiers' tents. Other councilors would have been insulted by such placement, but Aspen knew that Jaunty didn't concern himself with those things.

"As long as there is knowledge, monarchs will desire it," Jaunty had told Aspen once. "And thus I will always have a place at court, no matter how humble. I advise you to learn your lessons well. For even a Hostage Prince can become an advisor."

Good advice for then, Aspen thought bitterly, *useless now*.

❖ ❖ ❖

ONCE PAST THE sentries, Aspen had a clear path to Jaunty's tent. He guessed that most of the army was lined up on the plain and ready for battle, and what reserves had been left behind looked to be wholly concentrating on sharpening their weapons and making sure their armor had no blemishes.

Sudden cries from afar made him look around. *Skirmishers*, he thought, *restarting their hostilities. If I am to stop this war, I had better do it soon.*

With more speed than secrecy, he made for Jaunty's tent, hoping that if his concealment spells faltered, he would look like a spy heading to report.

As he neared the soldiers' area, he saw that most of those held back in reserve were Red Caps.

That makes sense, Aspen thought. Notoriously nearsighted, Red Caps would be fairly useless until dusk. But if the battle went long, an evening charge by the vicious little creatures could very well turn the tide.

Luckily, he reached the entrance to Jaunty's tent without incident. He had never known Jaunty to be on time for anything and hoped he was still running late.

If he is already with the rest of the councilors, I am finished.

Aspen listened at the tent flap for just a moment but heard nothing. Then he pushed the flap aside and went in.

The interior of the tent looked as if Jaunty had merely packed up his home chambers and moved everything he owned into the tent: his scarred old desk with the miniature pendulum on it, the crooked chair, the massive chest that housed his book collection and took an ogre's strength to open. As well as four of them to carry it the two times Jaunty had changed quarters to be nearer the king. A few of those books sat out on the desk: *Agarusk on Daylight Defense,* King Forund III's *Supplying the Horde,* and *Maneuvers* by the leader of the ancient Council of Koronog, whose name cannot be written as it is a very powerful rune that curses the viewer to a lifetime of hiccupping.

And there was Jaunty's warped old cot in the corner covered by a ratty woolen blanket with just a hint of white hair poking out from under it.

"Jaunty," Aspen hissed. There was no movement of the blanket, so he said louder, "Jaunty!"

This time the blanket flew off, and his former tutor sat up. He had always been old—Aspen had never known how old—but now he finally looked it. His dark skin was wrinkled, his back crooked, his two front teeth—fangs really—yellowed. With a wide grin, he whispered, "Prince Aspen! I am overjoyed that the reports of your death had been exaggerated."

The mere thought of someone being overjoyed to see him brought a tear to Aspen's eye. He lowered his tone to match Jaunty's whisper. "And I am happy to see you, too, Jaunty."

"What?"

"I said, I am happy to see you, too, Jaunty." Aspen spoke this time in a more normal tone.

"Quiet!" Jaunty hissed. "You are still a wanted prince, you know."

Aspen sighed. "Yes, I know. That's why I came. I know who is behind this war."

Jaunty sat up. Wiped a mottled claw through his thin hair. "Tell me."

So Aspen did. He told him about Old Jack Daw's plan to trick him into running away, and thus start a war. He told him about Snail and her bravery. He told him about Odds and his players and the battle at Bogsborough.

Jaunty sat silent, listening intently. "And I am supposed to take this to Obs? Tell him his most trusted advisor has betrayed him and misled him into war?" He snorted. "A war he is winning."

"Well . . ." Aspen hesitated.

Jaunty snorted again. "And quite enjoying, I might add."

When he puts it that way, my coming here does not sound like a very good plan. "I was hoping—"

"Hope," Jaunty said, "has dismal feathers and rarely flies." He looked at Aspen in that old familiar way. "Who wrote that?"

Aspen sighed. They had no time for this, but he said automatically, "The Border poet Malacom in his poem 'Hope Is a Feathered Thing.'"

"And you hold what dismal feathered hope, lad? That I would risk my life for you? You do not live to be my age by sticking your neck out for rash young princes." Jaunty stood. He had slept in his clothes and his armor, a strange combination of carapace and wood. He grabbed his walking stick. It was gnarled oak, twice his size. "But I will do it regardless."

"That is . . . um . . . great."

Jaunty smiled at him. If he meant it to be comforting, it missed by about six teeth's worth.

"You have truly never understood what being a scholar means, my dear boy." He shambled toward the tent flaps. "It means finding the truth and speaking it, no matter the consequences." He slid halfway through the flaps, then turned back. "Stay hidden, Prince Aspen Leaf. I shall return anon." And then he was gone.

Jaunty had ever called Aspen that when he was particularly pleased with him as a student. Somehow Aspen found it comforting that Jaunty, at least, had not changed. But he was suddenly exhausted beyond reckoning. He sat down on the cot and tried to remember the last time he'd slept. The camp was quieting as the Red Caps had obviously finished their preparations and had begun waiting. He wondered how long before they were called forth for their part in the coming battle.

According to his brother, waiting was the most common soldier's weapon. He recalled how fidgety he had been before being collected as the Hostage Prince. Not quite seven years old. His brother had come into his room and said, "Think of yourself as a Seelie soldier."

Aspen had whined, "I have no weapon. I am just waiting."

And his brother had said offhandedly—and it was the last thing he had said to Aspen before the delegates taking him to the Unseelie Court had arrived—"Soldiers learn how to wait. It is their most effective weapon, and their most dangerous."

So I wait, Aspen thought. *What else can I do? Besides, if Jaunty reaches the king, perhaps there will be no battle at all.*

Imagining *that* outcome, Aspen permitted himself a small smile. He thought about lying down and resting, but perhaps that was what his brother had meant about the danger.

If Jaunty settled things with Obs, he would once again be the Hostage Prince and could sleep in relative peace for the rest of his life, be it short or long.

It was the first time he actually realized that stopping the war would most likely come at the price of him returning to Obs's keep.

I am not ready to lose my freedom, he thought, suddenly afraid, even desperate. For a moment he imagined leaving the tent, heading back into the forest, though it would mean remaining on the run. And it would compromise Jaunty's life as well. So, he quickly quashed that coward's thought.

I pledged to do whatever it takes to stop the war. I cannot go back on that pledge.

As soon as he thought the word war, it sounded as if one started right outside the tent. Scampering to the flaps, he pulled one aside the tiniest bit and peered out. A large contingent of wolf-riders flying the red-splotch banner of King Obs was rushing into camp and heading for the king's tent.

The king's personal guards! I wonder what they are doing here.

The Red Caps clambered around, blocking Aspen's view, but he thought he saw the guards carrying a body into the king's tent.

Moments later Jaunty shuffled into his own tent, looking even more stooped than when he'd left.

"Did you speak to the king?" Aspen asked. "What has happened?"

Jaunty shook his head. "An assassin's arrow. In the back. The skin around the wound was blue, reeked of cinnamon."

"Cinnamon?" Aspen was confused. "And that means . . . ?"

"For Mab's sake, boy, did you not listen the days we discussed poisons? It was Witch Apple. There will be no recovery."

"Poison!" His head roiled with memories. *The dungeon master dead, the two assassins chasing him through the dungeons dead, the merman who tried to drag Snail out of the boat dead. All dead of poison.*

"King Obs dead?" he whispered.

That huge, overbearing presence that had ruled his life for the past six years gone? The king with the platter-sized right hand who swatted lesser fey dead as others would a fly? *So quickly. Without fanfare. Without hand-to-hand battle. Without the noble gesture.* He tried to believe it, failed, tried again.

Jaunty nodded.

"But . . . but . . . but . . ." Aspen sputtered. Suddenly he knew why he could barely speak. Obs had been his captor, but he had also been his only father for years. A father he largely hated and feared, but a father nonetheless. Aspen felt a hole open in his chest, and he wasn't sure how to fill it.

Mind racing, Aspen sighed. He would mourn Obs later. *Or not.* "Surely the queen will listen to you? Can you go to her . . . ?"

Jaunty looked at him strangely. "Oh, you have been away and never heard."

"Heard what?"

"The queen died in childbirth. The infant heir is now our liege lord."

"Oh." It took Aspen a moment to make the connection, see the pieces fall into place. The pieces that Old Jack Daw had laid on the board so long ago. "And his regent is?"

Jaunty nodded, knowing that Aspen had already guessed the answer. "Old Jack Daw."

Aspen stood speechless. Old Jack Daw had planned all of this: the war, the queen's death, the king's death. *The baby will never reach his majority either, I suppose. Jack did not just want war—he wanted the whole kingdom. And,* Aspen chewed on the bitter truth, *now he has it.*

"Fly, young Ailenbran," Jaunty said, alarmingly calling Aspen by his Seelie name. "Fly as far away as you can and never return. This land is lost to you now. I do not know where you shall find another."

Nor do I, Aspen thought, but could not bring himself to say it aloud.

Jaunty checked to see if the way was clear, then held up the back tent flap. Aspen stumbled out in a daze. Pulling the hood of his cloak over his head, he started trudging his way back up the hill under the cover of the trees.

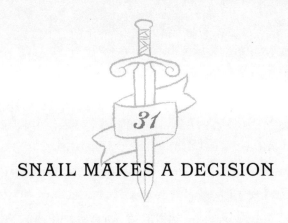

SNAIL MAKES A DECISION

$\mathcal{S}$nail turned over on the bed and woke slowly, disoriented and a bit muzzy and buzzy in her mind, as if a hive of bees had taken residence there. For a long moment she couldn't figure out where she was, and then when she had some of it figured out, she was alarmed.

She sat up too quickly and then felt so dizzy she lay back down again and reconstructed the last minutes she could: the search for Aspen, Odds's strange speech, a hand over her mouth, and a voice . . .

"Awake at last."

No, Snail thought, *not* that *voice*.

In fact, *that* voice belonged to Dagmarra, who was sitting on the bed across the room from her.

Snail had turned to look at the dwarf as Og—also on the bed—began to roll toward her, a dangerous thing except that Dagmarra put out a hand to stop him.

"How did I get here?" Snail asked. That was the part she couldn't remember.

"Why, Maggie Light brought you. Said you were exhausted from all the work you did around the camp, and getting little sleep out there, so she'd decided . . ."

"No!" Snail said, now remembering. "Maggie Light drugged me or something." She almost had it, and then it was gone again. Without thinking, she rubbed her right hand over her mouth and brought the back of her hand to her nose. There was the slightest odor of pine and honey. It was the smell that brought everything back into focus.

She sat up again, but carefully this time. "Said she was made . . ." She hesitated because she wanted to get it right. "She was made to do as she was told."

"*That* old excuse," Dagmarra said. "She hauls it out whenever she finds what she has to do in the slightest bit distasteful."

It was not Maggie Light's excuse but the sourness in Snail's mouth that was distasteful, but she didn't remark upon it. Instead she said, "I was looking for Karl."

"The prince? You know he's been gone two days already. And good riddance, I say."

"How can you say that after what he did for Huldra and Og!" Dagmarra bristled at her tone, but Snail didn't care. "He fought for them, hunted for them, risked his life for the child *you* now raise!"

"He did fight well," Dagmarra agreed, none too graciously.

"More than that. He fought *nobly*." Snail was surprised

that tears were running out of her eyes as quickly as if they were late for appointments. "I *have* to find him."

Dagmarra grumbled something. Looked uncomfortable.

"What? What did you say?" Snail said.

"I hate it when girls cry," Dagmarra said. "It's just what people expect. Stop it and I'll think of something. For you, if not for him."

Snail snuffled up her tears, wiped her face with a sleeve. "Done," she said.

Dagmarra took out her pipe and, while she didn't smoke it when inside the wagon, she sucked on it. The sound was somehow soothing. "With three different armies tromping about, you won't be able to walk there," she said at last. "Wherever *there* is."

"Well, I sure can't *fly*," Snail said. It came out angrier than she meant.

"But the bowser can," said Dagmarra. "Which is why we keep him here, chained inside the wagon. Trouble is not to get him flying, it's to get him flying where you want him to go. He's got a mind of his own."

"The rug is a he?"

Dagmarra nodded.

"How do you know?"

"Well, that's a wee bit tricky. First you—"

"Wait," Snail said, "he *flies*?"

Dagmarra nodded again. "His mother was a simple rag

rug but his father was a flying carpet. The main problem is, he doesn't like females."

Snail thought about after the battle, when the bowser seemed to take comfort from her presence after all the terrifying noise. "I'll manage."

"We'll be needing Maggie Light for this," Dagmarra told her.

"But she was the one who . . ."

"Without her help, you have no chance."

"Well there's always the chance that she'll tell Odds."

"You'll have to take that chance," Dagmarra told her. "It's the only one you've got. Here, watch the baby, I'll get Mags."

Snail sat on the bed next to Og, who slept restlessly, his legs twitching, his thumb continually seeking his mouth yet never quite finding it.

Snail put a hand lightly on his back to keep him still, and counted the seconds until Dagmarra came back with Maggie Light. It took a count of five hundred sixty-seven. Each second felt like the toll of the castle bell when a member of the royal family died.

When she saw them, Snail stood up. Og began to roll about the bed, which made Dagmarra rush to his side.

Snail glared at Maggie Light, but she shrugged it off.

"I would be sorry, but I cannot," Maggie Light said. She continued without pause. "Come into the other room,

Sofie-Snail, and we will set the bowser free. You do that, and he may even let you on his back."

Snail hesitated. "Will you tell the professor what I plan to do?"

"I will have to," Maggie Light said. "It is how I am made. But not soon. I have an internal clock I can dismantle for a bit until he notices it and sets me aright. That can give you several hours' start. It may be enough."

It was the repetition of the word *made* that finally penetrated Snail's fog.

Made? Snail thought. *Does she really mean she's a* made *thing? Not a human or fey woman at all, but like the mechanical spiders and the various strange tools on Odds's desk?* Suddenly—like the puzzle Odds had set her to take apart and put together again—everything fell into place.

"I understand you must do as Odds tells you," she told Maggie Light. "But when you act on your own, you have more caring in you than many a true person."

"Maybe that is because the professor made me in the image of his mother," Maggie Light said. "See?" She held up her arms and the draped sleeve fell away. In her armpit there was a stamped name. It began with an M. "Her name was Margaret Lightson. She was a singer and died young. I will never die. Though I may run down. Or rust."

"What's rust?" Snail asked.

"A natural process in which iron turns to—"

"You are made of iron? But . . ."

"Only my armature," Maggie Light said.

Snail was confused. Maggie Light's arms looked perfectly fine to her. But before she could say so, Maggie Light continued.

"Thanks really go to Dagmarra. Her arguments about helping you have been persuasive." Maggie Light looked over at the dwarf, who had settled back on the bed, one hand now on Og's belly to steady him.

"What did she say?" asked Snail.

"That we women have to be for one another when no one else will be for us. And that includes the professor and both of Dagmarra's brothers."

❖ ❖ ❖

THEY WENT INTO the next room, where the twins stood guard over the bowser. The rug growled when Snail came close, and so she retreated. But only as far as the door.

Maggie Light spoke a poem about flying and compassion and something else. Or it might have been about freedom. Not that the words actually said any of that specifically, but the words *under* the words did. Or at least that was how it seemed to Snail.

The way is long, the night is deep,
The hills are high, the valleys steep,

And you have promises to keep,
Be not a liar.

The day is short, the rider light,
The war is sharp, the battle tight,
The need is great, the moment right,
My trusty flier.

The bowser shook itself all over, like a dog, and the growl seemed to lessen just a bit.

A bit is better than a bite, Snail thought.

"Come over here now," Maggie Light called to Snail.

She came, but cautiously.

The bowser roused himself as if to examine her. She could see his mouth, the teeth now carefully shielded, but he had no eyes. She wondered how he could tell who she was.

"Rider, bowser." Maggie Light's voice was soft but steel. "Bowser, rider."

Feeling slightly foolish, Snail nodded at the rug.

The rug didn't nod back, but he did stop growling.

"Sit on him, pet him," Maggie Light said, "and tell him how beautiful he is. He is easily flattered."

Snail sat. The bowser felt like a rug except for the occasional ripples beneath her. *Like a horse*, she thought, *with little runnels of fear. Or anger.*

"You are a beauty," she whispered. "I am honored that

you will let me ride with you." *"With" not "on,"* she thought, *is better. Makes us equals. I must remember to tell that to Aspen. If the bowser lifts me. If I find Aspen. If I do not fall off along the way.*

"Now get off and we will take the bowser outside," Maggie said. "The front end of the wagon, not the back; less likely that the professor will see us."

She and Maggie and the bowser went first, the bowser hunching awkwardly along the ground. The strange twins in their long black capes were next, moving as if they were boneless. Last came Dagmarra with the drooling Og.

Seven of us. A crowd. Snail's worries increased. *We're sure to make a stir. This isn't a good idea. But as it's Maggie Light directing this play, there's no use arguing how many actors are in it.*

"Here," said Dagmarra, holding the baby on her shoulder with one hand and digging into her leather pocket with the other. She pulled out a handful of dandelion fluff. "For your ears."

Snail knew the drill by now. Quickly, she rolled the fluff into two plugs and stuffed them in her ears. Then she sat down again on the bowser, remembering to praise him profusely, for his nap, his color, his acceptance of their flight together.

Maggie began to sing again, not for the bowser, but a song that kept any human clan folk from noticing them, with a chorus that directed, "Look down, look down, look down."

Snail could just barely hear it through the earplugs and still had to work to raise her own eyes to the skies.

Dagmarra came close and said—loud enough for Snail to hear—"Hold tight to the bowser's fur; steer with your mind."

"Steer where?"

"You will know," Dagmarra said. "And if you do not, the bowser likely will."

Snail lay down on her stomach, stretching to her full length on the bowser and grabbing handfuls of his fur with her fingers, all the while saying her praises of the rug's beauty, his good sense and the sweetness of his temper (she hoped), as well as his generosity in letting her ride on his back. *At least,* she thought, *I hope this is his back.*

The first lift upward so startled her, she almost fell off. She yanked at the fur, and the bowser showed his teeth to her. They were right next to her face.

Fearing the bowser would buck her off like an angry horse, she loosened her grip slightly, but didn't dare let go. She didn't dare look down, either, but pressed herself even closer to the bowser, if that was possible, burying her face in his fur. He smelled clean and soapy and made her think of Aspen, whose task it had been to wash the rug.

❖ ❖ ❖

As THEY GAINED altitude, the temperature began to drop and Snail was almost able to convince herself that her shaking was due to the cold.

Almost.

The bowser sailed along, occasionally dipping to the right or left to catch a passing wind-stream. Snail could feel the change in his speed at those moments and a kind of unspoken joy rushed through her.

Soon she felt comfortable and safe enough to look about to the left and right whenever they flew along the valleys.

Eventually, she even enjoyed leaning over the edge of the bowser and looking straight down, catching her breath at the beauty that lay below. She loved it when they followed the silver ribbon of a river that seemed to wind on forever. And loved it when they skimmed the tops of trees, startling battalions of birds from their nests.

She discovered she adored passing through the wispy, low clouds on the mountains. And once, banking near a high crag, she saw an eagle in its aerie, and the bowser flew close enough so she could have put out a hand and snatched a feather but didn't dare.

Snail knew that after this ride, she would forever envy birds their wings and miss the feel of wind rushing through her hair. That is, if she had a forever.

And thinking that, she was brought back to the war that, for much of the ride, had somehow been far from her thoughts.

❖ ❖ ❖

WHETHER SNAIL WAS guiding the bowser with her mind or he was simply on his own flight path, she was never to know for sure. But later that evening, just as the sun was going down behind the highest peaks and dusk spread its orange cloak across the sky, the bowser suddenly banked and headed down, like a hawk in its perilous stoop.

"Wait!" she cried. "Where are you going? Why are we going down?" But the wind snatched the words from her mouth and she was holding on too tightly and was too frightened by the precipitous fall to steer with her mind.

Even if she had known how.

In the end, after a short glide across an empty glade, the bowser slid to a stop. He rose slightly and dumped Snail off. She landed in some high grass that cushioned her as she tumbled along.

She'd no idea where they were, but evidently the bowser did, because he scrunched along the grass toward a copse of trees as if he knew something she didn't.

Snail hurried after because she dared not lose sight of the rug.

Suddenly, the bowser rose up and wrapped himself around one particular tree, shaking it like a boy trying to shake apples off a bough.

Something large fell out of the tree, and the bowser caught it expertly.

"Stand aside," a familiar voice shouted. "Let me go!"

"Your high and mightiness," Snail called, "the bowser's found you. He probably thinks you're his master."

"It's a he?" Aspen said, standing.

Snail nodded.

"How do you know?"

"Maggie Light told me."

"Well it . . . er, he . . . has nearly killed me," Aspen said. "And I am no one's master."

"What were you doing in the tree?"

"Scouting," he said. "Though it is rousingly difficult. There are two armies out there, and only one me."

"Now there are two of us, Prince. *Plus* the bowser." Snail smiled into the darkness. "And he flies."

ASPEN OVERSEES THE BATTLE

$\mathcal{A}$spen had so many questions to ask Snail. *How did you find me? Did Odds send you? Have you forgiven me? Are we still friends?* But all he said was, "It flies?" The doubt in his voice was palpable.

Snail nodded and laughed. Aspen was so relieved that he almost forgot their situation.

Almost.

"We must leave," he said. "Immediately."

"But I must tell you about Odds." She frowned deeply. "We have a third army to stop."

Aspen shook his head. "Tell me in the air." He looked doubtfully down at the bowser, which was rubbing against his leg. He said again, even more doubtfully this time, "It . . . er . . . he flies?"

"Get on," Snail commanded. "Hold tight. Watch the horizon."

He sat down cross-legged in front of her the same way

she sat, knees drawn up. He grabbed two handfuls of the bowser's fur, thinking, *Not possible.*

Snail put her right hand on his right shoulder.

For a moment he thought to reprimand her. But only for a moment, for the bowser shuddered beneath him, began to lift, then rose straight up into the air.

The air, he thought, suddenly realizing that there was nothing now between him and earth but colorless, unseen air. He looked down at the ground suddenly rushing away beneath him and felt something like a boulder drop into his stomach.

"The horizon," came Snail's steady voice. "Watch the horizon."

He looked up, saw the familiar thin line where land and sky met, and was glad of Snail's hand.

"Those who are meant to fly are given wings," he muttered. "And elves are not so blessed."

"What?" Snail asked, then—without waiting for an answer—said, "We have to stop the battle! Odds has an army and is going to attack the winner of the battle when they're weakest."

Aspen stared straight ahead, trying not to think about how far up they were, how fast they had gotten there. "The winner won't be weak," he managed at last.

"Why not?"

"Because Old Jack Daw will not have left anything to chance."

Aspen felt her hand tighten on his shoulders at the mention of the old drow.

"Look," she said, and pointed ahead of him and down.

He peered over the edge of the bowser, trying to ignore the feeling that he was going to tip over it. The bowser had returned them to Aspen's perch of yesterday, where he had first looked down and seen the Seelie and Unseelie forces on the plain.

The two armies were still there, though they looked more like one army now, for they had closed the distance between them. Infantry clashed at the center, while bolts of lightning and balls of fire screamed over the ranks.

There were creatures in the air as well, though well below the bowser—harpies and dragonets—but they had to dodge arrows in the spell-filled sky. Luckily the bowser sailed far above both arrows and magic.

The sounds of screams and explosions, of weapons clashing, all drifted up the mountainside, though at this distance they were barely louder than the dawn chorus of birds had been. Aspen tried to make out the colors of banners, the movement of troops, but it was hopeless.

He had no idea who was winning.

"There!" Snail said, pointing at a flurry of activity to one side. "Is that your father's cavalry?"

Aspen looked where she pointed and saw a large troop of cavalry moving away from the main hostilities toward their enemy's left flank.

"No one else has any, so yes, it must be."

He watched, trying to discern the meaning of the maneuver.

Does my father flee?

It seemed unlikely. But Jaunty had always said that in war the bravest men sometimes do the most cowardly things and cowardly men the bravest. Thinking of Jaunty brought back memories of his long hours studying battle strategy, and suddenly he saw a magic smoke spell between the armies fizzle out. There was a groan from his father's soldiers. But then the groan turned to a cheer.

That is so *brilliant!* Aspen thought.

"Oh, Aspen, I'm so sorry the spell failed," Snail said into his ear.

It seemed clear that—outnumbered, and forced to attack or be overrun in the night—his father had thrown the bulk of his force at the center of the Unseelie lines. It looked like a hopeless attack, providing a lot of chaos and confusion. But what Aspen realized at once was that the failed fireball spell had thrown up a wall of smoke screening the cavalry from view as they wheeled right and made for the enemy's rear.

He turned his head and said to Snail, "In fact the spell didn't fail. It did what it was supposed to do—smoked and fizzled on purpose."

"What?" Snail sounded puzzled.

Aspen assumed it was because, as a girl and a servant, she

had never had the opportunity to study the strategy and rules for war. And there was no time to explain it all to her. But as he watched in awe, the cavalry gained the high ground *behind* the enemy, then pointed their lances downhill.

And then they began to charge.

"Oh my!" Snail exclaimed, lifting her hand off Aspen's shoulder. "Is your father actually going to win?"

"A skirmish," he said, quoting Jaunty, "is not a battle, and a battle is not the war." But he kept on grinning at what was unfolding below.

A small group of Red Caps were quickly scattered without slowing the charge, and then the lancers raised up in their saddles ready to hit the main army. In theory, they could— he knew—split the Unseelie forces down the middle and break them. But as Jaunty often said, "Theory and practice, difficult neighbors, uncomfortable friends."

"I think—"

Just then, the lead horse faltered and fell, throwing its rider aside. The other horses reined in and the nearest riders dismounted. They grabbed the rider from the ground and slung him over a horse's rump. Then they remounted and all turned, galloping straight away from the fight.

And just like that, the battle was over. The Seelie center broke and ran, making for camp as if that would offer them protection.

The flank farthest from the wooded hillside threw down their weapons, but apparently surrender was not an option.

They were ridden down by dire wolves and kelpies who slaughtered them where they stood.

The nearer flank made for the woods, but none reached the trees without at least one arrow in them. Most never made it that far.

Exhausted wizards were plucked up by harpies, who made great sport of dropping them from on high. Those with any juice left waved their hands in frantic, mystic passes and popped out of sight.

Fleeing soldiers met the reserves in camp, and they began to fight each other over the few carts and horses they thought to escape on. When the Unseelie army arrived moments later, there was no resistance, only more slaughter.

Difficult neighbors, indeed, Aspen thought, his eyes filling with tears.

Terrible neighbors.

The worst.

And who should know better than he, having lived so long among them.

The bowser whined and Aspen finally tore his gaze away. The wind was suddenly cold on his face, and he realized he was weeping. He raised his hand to wipe his face and stopped. His fingers tingled; his palms were wreathed in a golden aura.

No! he thought. *Not Father! No wonder the cavalry turned and ran. With his body.*

"Odds is here!" Snail shouted over the noise Aspen dimly recognized as his own wracking sobs.

To the west of the destroyed Seelie camp a line of giant spiders was just stepping out from the concealment of the trees, their metal carapaces gleaming in the morning sun. Thousands of motley humans gathered around their legs, armed and eager, if not well organized.

Enough, Aspen thought, *to run right through the depleted Seelie army had the cavalry charge actually hit home and destroyed the greater Unseelie army.*

He shook his head and wiped the last of the tears from his eyes. *My father never had a chance today.*

A horn blasted from the nearer camp and the Unseelie army lined up to face the new threat, looking large and professional and not overly tired.

Odds has no chance either if he attacks now, Aspen thought.

The professor seemed to have the same thought, and the human army disappeared back into the woods as quickly as it had come.

"Take us down," Aspen said.

He felt Snail stiffen behind him. "Are you mad? We need to fly away. Now!"

"Take us down!" Aspen shouted, and the bowser obeyed, diving swiftly but pulling up at the last moment to settle gently in a bed of pine needles.

Aspen rolled off the bowser and turned to face Snail.

Her face, which had been red and angry, was suddenly blanched white. "What's happening to you?" she asked.

The golden aura so recently tickling his palms had now spread to his arms, and a slight burning sensation came with it. *Not unpleasant, though,* he thought. Soon it would spread to his entire body. Not a disease, but a dis-ease of spirit, of necessity. He had read about it, but never seen it of course.

He spoke plainly to Snail. "My father is dead. Most likely my brothers as well." He was glad to have stopped weeping. This was a moment that should be handled with dignity and—perhaps—hope, though at the moment, hope seemed very far away.

"You don't know that, Aspen," Snail said. "They may have survived the battle."

The glow moved to his chest now, and he felt it inside.

"Actually, I do." He put his arms to his sides, bracing himself for what came next. "In the Unseelie Court," he went on, "succession is decided by primacy: the oldest male child of the current monarch takes over when he dies."

"What does—"

"Which usually makes for a lot of dead male children." He smiled at Snail, but the look on her face told him it was much more of a grimace than a grin. "However, in the Seelie Court the land chooses its own king. Usually by primacy—which is why my brothers have most likely perished—though not always. But my father has certainly died."

His whole body glowed gold now, and he knew by the yellowing of his vision that soon his head would, too.

"But *how* can you know?" Snail asked.

Before he could speak, the golden aura encased his head and he felt it enter him fully.

I am Faery.

I am silent stone and rumbling rivers. I am shifting sands and tumbling rocks. I am woodlands and grasslands and the caverns below. I am the mythic isles and the water around. I am the river of blood and the broken hedge. I am the scarred plain defiled by darkness. The darkness pierced by the thorns.

I am Faery.

"Because the land has chosen me," Aspen said. "For good, for bad, for the length of my life, I am now the Seelie king."

Snail gasped and froze for a moment, then hurriedly began to duck down into a deep curtsy.

Aspen reached out a hand to stop her. "No."

A part of him could not believe that he was telling a human, a *servant*, not to bow. But it was a very small part, and easy to ignore.

"Never bow to me, Snail. I am not your liege. I am your friend." He thought that he sounded very kingly, but then ruined it by continuing in a rush. "At least I think I am. Are we still friends? I hope so. I did not mean to leave you behind, but you would not speak to me because of the changeling thing and—I had no one else . . ."

"Of course we're still friends, stupid." There were tears on Snail's face now, too, and he wasn't sure why.

Aspen drew himself up and pretended offense, but he was grinning too hard for it to be believable. "I do not think you should call a king stupid."

"Don't ask stupid questions, then."

"Fair enough." He puffed his chest out and spoke loudly. "Herefore and henceforth and from this day forward, Snail the Midwife shall not have to perform me any obeisance and may call me 'stupid' and 'muddle-minded' and 'dunderhead' or any designation of her choosing if I have, in her opinion, acted in a stupid, muddle-minded, or otherwise idiotic manner." He nodded at her. "There, I have made my first decree as king. I hope I live long enough to make it into law."

Snail barked a short laugh that had little feel of humor in it, then cocked her head to one side, listening.

Aspen heard it, too: a mass of people moving up the mountain, no doubt Unseelie soldiers searching for survivors.

"And possibly your last decree if we don't get out of here," she said.

Fresh tears sprang to his eyes. He wiped them away harshly, steeling himself.

I have no time for sadness, now. I am king. He stepped onto the bowser. *Not much of a start to my reign, fleeing from battle with only a changeling and an animate rug.* However, all he said aloud was, "I need my friends around me now."

She smiled tentatively. "Guess I'm it."

He smiled back, in what he assumed was a kingly manner. "Guess you are," he said, holding out a golden hand and pulling her onto the rug with him.

They rose into the sky as the golden aura faded from around him and settled deep in his chest.

I am Ailenbran Astaeri, Bright Celestial, Ruire of the Tir na nOg, and Lord of the Seelie kingdom.

I have promises not yet kept. Friends not yet made. Enemies not yet met. Mourning not yet begun.

I am Faery.

And I am at war.

END OF BOOK TWO OF THE SEELIE WARS TRILOGY

WWW.THESEELIEWARS.COM

JANE YOLEN, called "the Hans Christian Andersen of America" (*Newsweek*) and the "Aesop of the Twentieth Century" (*The New York Times*), is the author of well over three hundred books, including *Owl Moon, The Devil's Arithmetic,* and the How Do Dinosaurs . . . series. Her work ranges from rhymed picture books and baby board books through middle grade fiction, poetry collections, and nonfiction, and up to novels and story collections for young adults and adults. She has also written lyrics for folk-rock singers and groups, and several animated shorts. She's done voiceover work and talk radio. Her books and stories have won an assortment of awards—two Nebulas, a World Fantasy Award, a Caldecott Medal, the Golden Kite Award, three Mythopoeic Awards, two Christopher Medals, a nomination for the National Book Award, and the Jewish Book Award, among others. She has been nominated three times for the Pushcart Prize. She is also the winner of the World Fantasy Association's Lifetime Achievement Award, the Science Fiction Poetry Association's Grand Master Award, the Catholic Library's Regina Medal, the Kerlan Award from the University of Minnesota, the 2012 de Grummond Medal, and the Smith College Alumnae Medal. Six colleges and universities have given her honorary doctorates.

Also worthy of note, she lost her fencing foil in Grand Central Station on a date and fell overboard while white-water rafting in the Colorado River, and her Skylark Award—given to her by NESFA, the New England Science Fiction Association—set her good coat on fire. If you need to know more about her, visit her website at www.janeyolen.com.

ADAM STEMPLE is an author, musician, web designer, maker of book trailers, and professional card player. He has published many short stories, and CDs and tapes of his music, as well as seven fantasy novels—five for middle graders and two for adults. One of his middle grade novels, *Pay the Piper* (also written with Jane Yolen), won the 2006 *Locus* Award for Best Young Adult Book. The *Locus* plaque sits on the shelf next to two Minnesota Music Awards and trophies from his Fall Poker Classic and All In Series wins. His first adult novel, *Singer of Souls*, was described by Anne McCaffrey as "one of the best first novels I have ever read." For musings, music downloads, code snippets, and writing advice, visit him at www.adamstemple.com.

Nov 2014